DEAD ON ARRIVAL

A DCI JAMES CRAIG NOVEL

JOHN CARSON

DCI James Craig series
Ice Into Ashes
One of the Broken
Dead on Arrival
Whisper of Guilt

DCI HARRY MCNEIL SERIES

Return to Evil
Sticks and Stones
Back to Life
Dead Before You Die
Hour of Need
Blood and Tears
Devil to Pay
Point of no Return
Rush to Judgement
Against the Clock
Fall from Grace
Crash and Burn
Dead and Buried
All or Nothing
Never go Home
Famous Last Words
Do Unto Others
Twist of Fate
Now or Never
Blunt Force Trauma

CALVIN STEWART SERIES
Final Warning
Hard Case

DCI SEAN BRACKEN SERIES
Starvation Lake
Think Twice
Crossing Over
Life Extinct
Over Kill

DI FRANK MILLER SERIES
Crash Point
Silent Marker
Rain Town
Watch Me Bleed
Broken Wheels
Sudden Death
Under the Knife
Trial and Error
Warning Sign
Cut Throat
Blood from a Stone
Time of Death

Frank Miller Crime Series – Books 1-3 – Box set
Frank Miller Crime Series - Books 4-6 - Box set

MAX DOYLE SERIES
Final Steps
Code Red
The October Project

SCOTT MARSHALL SERIES

Old Habits

DEAD ON ARRIVAL

Copyright © 2024
John Carson

www.johncarsonauthor.com

John Carson has asserted his right under the Copyright, Designs and Patents Act 1988, to be identified as the author of this work.

This is a work of fiction. Names, characters, places, brands, media, and incidents are either the products of the author's imagination or are used fictitiously. Any resemblance to actual events, locales, or persons, living or dead, is coincidental.

Without limiting the rights under copyright reserved above, no part of this publication may be reproduced, stored in or introduced into a retrieval system, or transmitted, in any form, or by any means (electronic, mechanical, photocopying, recording, or otherwise) without the prior written permission of the author of this book. Innocence is and

All rights reserved

 Created with Vellum

For my friend Spence.
Just you, me and the chiropractor.
Nobody will ever know.

ONE

'Sometimes I hate this fucking place.' Pathologist Annie Keller slumped back against the service lift and took out a cigarette.

DCI James Craig smiled at her. 'You should try sucking something when you feel the need to have a ciggie.'

Annie raised her eyebrows. 'Got any suggestions?'

He took out a packet of Polo mints and offered her one.

'Despite the fact it has pocket lint on it, I'll take one.' She took the round mint and popped it in her mouth and put her cigarette away.

'Why do you keep a packet on you?' Craig asked her.

'Same reason my dad kept a bottle of whisky in the toilet cistern.'

'Fair enough,' he replied as the lift stopped at the dungeon level. They stepped out into a windowless corridor and walked along to the mortuary, Annie in her tan-coloured trousers and white blouse, Craig still wearing his lightweight jacket, feeling his sweat gathering the troops in his armpits despite his having liberally spraying his body with deodorant that the advertising promised him would make him more macho and handsome, both of which failed to materialise.

Annie crunched the mint and swallowed. 'So much for sucking it. I can eat a whole packet of those things in one go. Keeping my dentist in a job.'

Craig held them out for her. 'Keep them.'

'Usually, a man will bring me flowers and chocolates.'

'We're not dating.'

'You take the fun out of everything, Jimmy Craig.'

Annie was two years younger than Craig's forty-seven but didn't look her age.

'I don't think my wife spiking my coffee with antifreeze is fun.'

'You think that's the route she would take if we had an affair and she found out?'

'That or pills. Maybe arsenic.'

'The favourite method for women to kill men.' She smiled at him. 'We could drive all night. Nobody would know.'

Craig wasn't sure if she meant it or not but smiled at her. Annie was divorced, and she needed a man in her life, he thought. 'How's the love life?' he asked her.

'Jesus, you're a fast worker. You give me a mint and the next thing you're suggesting we start seeing each other. I'll give you credit, though; that body spray you're wearing should be called Big Shagger.'

'That would certainly be a better name than Thor's Ball-bag.'

She looked at him for a second. 'Christ, you had me going there.' She swiped her card at the double doors, which opened inwards, and they walked through to the mortuary.

'To answer your question, I'm that close to pulling the trigger on getting a cat.' Her thumb and index finger were almost touching.

'Nothing wrong with that. Isla has a cat.' DS Isla McGregor, one of Craig's colleagues.

'I know. Mr Boots. I'm on his Christmas card list. We're almost exchanging birthday cards.'

'What's stopping you?' Craig grinned.

'I refuse to tell anybody when my birthday is. If he finds out, I've chosen a country I can flee to that doesn't have an extradition treaty with the UK.'

'I won't tell,' Craig said.

'You don't know when it is.'

'Of course I do: August 1st.'

'That's creepy. Now I'm having visions of you breaking into my house and raking through my knicker drawer.' She put a hand to her mouth before letting it fall to her side. 'Crap. I just revealed where I keep my address book with birthdays in it.'

'I hope mine is in there.'

'Of course it is. But seriously, how do you know when my birthday is? Did you run my name through your system or something?'

'You told me one Saturday night when you were pished.'

She narrowed her eyes. 'When was that?'

'Two weeks ago. Dan and I were having a pint, and you popped into the golf club and decided to try and break the world record for drinking the most amount of alcohol in the least amount of time.'

'Did I call Isla to come and get me?'

'You did. And she did.'

'God, I can't even remember getting home.'

'Isla took care of you after you told me when your birthday is.'

'I need to stop consuming alcohol,' she said.

'Maybe just cut back on chugging tequila.'

They stopped at her office and she unlocked the door and they stepped inside. It was cool in here; the mortuary itself was kept at an even temperature.

'I haven't had a drink since that night,' she said.

'I believe you.'

'People who *don't* believe you say exactly that,' Annie said. 'But it's true.'

Craig saw a shift in her demeanour. 'You want to talk about it?'

She picked up a book from a bookcase behind her desk and handed it to him. 'Tell Eve she can keep it.'

'Thanks, I will. But you didn't ask me along here this morning to pick up a book before we start work.'

She sighed. 'I suppose that's why you're the detective.'

He waited patiently as she looked at him.

'I have a stalker.' She held up a hand as he was

about to speak. 'Ninety per cent sure. Not a hundred, but I'm scared, Jimmy. That's why I've stayed sober. I'm on the verge of getting not only a cat but a big fuck-off Rottweiler.'

'Have you told anybody else?' Craig asked.

'That I'm a paranoid weirdo about to become a cat lady? I don't think so.'

'You're not paranoid; you're just conscious about your personal safety.' He wasn't patronising her, and she could tell he was being genuine. 'Have you told anybody else about this?' he asked again.

She shook her head. 'Just you. I wasn't sure at first. It was just a feeling of being watched.'

'Did you see him sitting in a car watching your house?'

'No. I looked, trust me. But I've been getting phone calls at home and he's hanging up.'

'It's somebody who knows you enough to have found out your phone number. If it's not a number you need, unplug your home phone.'

Annie nodded. 'I've also had gifts and letters through the mail.'

Craig looked at her. 'Like what?'

'Flowers. Chocolates. A teddy bear. No Polo mints, though.'

'How long have you been divorced?' Craig asked.

'Two years.'

'Has your ex bothered you before?'

Annie thought about it. 'It wasn't the easiest divorce in the world. He was a complete bastard, to be honest. He calls me up in the middle of the night when he's drunk, berating me.'

'Where does he live now?'

'Edinburgh. We lived together in Dunfermline, but he moved. He's a surgeon and he transferred to the Royal Infirmary over there.'

'Do you think he could be behind this?' Craig asked.

'I don't know. He's moved on now. Shagging a nurse, last I heard. Younger, fitter, and as Alanis Morissette asked, will she go down on him in a theatre?' She looked at Craig. 'Not that I ever did that, mind. Fuck, no. I'd have slapped the shit out of him if he'd asked me to do that, but I have friends over there and the word is, this nurse is a little... flighty, as my old mother used to say.' Tears sprang into her eyes, and then she started crying, and grabbed hold of Craig, who put his arms around her.

Between sobs, Annie told him, 'I miss my mum so much. She's been gone a long time and I miss her every day. I wish I could call her up and talk to her.'

She pulled apart from Craig and looked into his

eyes. 'I wish young people who still have their parents would call them up and tell them they love them instead of waiting until they're gone and wishing they could spend one more day with them.'

'I agree.' He held her at arm's length as if she would keel over at any minute.

'What's your ex-husband's name?' he asked her.

'Montgomery Price. Monty to his friends.'

Craig let her arms go.

'Thanks, Jimmy. I needed that. Sometimes being single again is a real bitch. Christ, I'm in my forties and left to do online dating or meet some bastard who wants to cheat on his wife.'

'I can't pretend I know what that's like. And I won't patronise you and say there's somebody for everybody. You might never find that right person.'

She sniffed and laughed. 'You're a barrel of laughs.'

'I mean, there *is* somebody for everybody, even you,' he said.

'Even me? Like I'm Quasimodo's sister? Thanks, Jimmy.'

'You know what I mean. I'm no good at this shite.'

She laughed again. 'Sometimes I just need a shoulder to cry on.'

'You can cry on mine anytime.'

'Thank you. It's not true what they say about you.'

He smiled. 'I think it is.'

TWO

Given that it was summertime in Scotland, there was the obligatory drizzle when Craig arrived at the cemetery in Burntisland. Other police vehicles were parked outside the main gate, but a uniform waved him through when he showed his warrant card.

There were more vehicles inside, including a mortuary van. Craig had driven over from the hospital with his foot to the floor, and Annie had left a microsecond after him, but he could see her Audi already parked ahead.

He stepped out of his car and grabbed a raincoat from the boot and shrugged it on, walking towards the caretaker's house.

DS Dan Stevenson walked towards him. 'Morning, boss.'

'Morning, Dan. What do we have here?'

'A young woman found sitting against a gravestone. Cut across her throat. And something else. You can see for yourself.'

The house was stone built and would have been worth a lot of money if it hadn't been hiding in a cemetery. The place itself was well kept, like a park with dead people buried in it.

'Who found her?' Craig asked as they walked along towards the forensics tent.

'A drunk guy being chased by a patrol officer for having a pish in the street.'

'What about the caretaker?' Craig asked.

'He's knocking on the door to retirement. First he knew was the Uniforms banging on his door.'

'Where is he now?'

'In his house. Isla's taking a statement and talking to him and his wife.'

Craig nodded as he saw Annie Keller, dressed in her white suit, coming out of the tent that had been erected around the body.

'What kept you?' she asked as he approached her. She was grinning, obviously all thoughts of some mad bastard stalking her shelved for the moment.

'I took the scenic route,' he said. 'You know,

stopped for a coffee, had an ice cream while I walked along the promenade.'

'Aw, you're such a bad loser. You're just mad because I beat you here.'

'You would beat James Hunt if he was racing you here. And alive of course, God rest his soul.'

'Talking of James Hunt, here's Mark Baker.'

Craig turned to look at the detective superintendent walking towards them. He wasn't wearing a raincoat and looked even more dishevelled than he normally did.

'I think he's been watching too many *Columbo* reruns,' Annie said.

'Columbo wore a raincoat. I'm going for Cannon.'

'Cannon was overweight. Baker could do with a good meal,' Annie said.

'There has to be some skinny, scruffy bastard TV detective he's modelling himself on.'

'I'm going for Morse. Even though he was older,' Dan said.

'Nah, Morse had better stature than Baker,' Craig said.

'Right then,' Baker said as he got closer to them. 'Starsky and Hutch. Oh, and let's not forget Dr Quincy there.' Baker was out of breath, his suit looked like a dog had slept on it, and his hair had valiantly fought the hairbrush that morning and won although the DSup kept his hair relatively short.

'See? I told you the quiz night would come back to bite us in the arse,' Annie said. 'Bloody seventies detectives.' She looked at Dan. '*Morse* wasn't on in the seventies.'

'I stand corrected.'

'How are you this morning, Mark?' Annie said to Baker. 'I only ask because you look like utter shite.'

'Thanks, Annie. I can always rely on you for a morning pep talk.'

She grinned at him. 'Go on, I'll let you have one back.' She held out her arms. 'Give it your best shot.'

'You look like an overweight polar bear.'

Annie dropped her arms to her sides and let her mouth drop open. 'Overweight? Where the fuck did that come from? This paper suit is baggy, that's all.'

'Oh, aye, I meant just…polar bear.'

'Sod off. That's the last time I'm going to let you get away with anything like that.'

Baker dug his hands into his pockets, shrugged his shoulders up and looked at Craig for help.

'Don't look at me, boss. You're the one who just called her a fat bastard.'

'No, he didn't,' Annie said, skelping his arm. 'He

used the term "overweight", which could mean a few pounds.' She looked at Baker. 'That *is* what you meant, isn't it? A few pounds?'

He looked at her and nodded. 'Aye, aye, that's what I meant.' He looked at Craig and mouthed, *Bastard*.

'Right then, moving on,' Annie said, tutting and shaking her head. 'Allow me to give you the tour.' She stepped inside the tent and the three officers followed.

The grass around the headstone was dry but probably felt damp, not that the girl was noticing. She was dressed in jeans and a golf polo shirt. Her head was resting on her right shoulder, like she had fallen asleep and tilted over, which, in the living, would have stiffened the muscles, but this girl wasn't going to feel anything.

Blood had run down from her neck onto her shirt, staining the front of it.

'I'd say this was the cause of death,' Annie said, pointing in the general direction of the girl's throat.

'Any ID on her?' Baker asked.

'Stan Mackay is creeping about here somewhere,' Annie said, 'and he said there was nothing in her pockets. They took her fingerprints and we'll see if something comes back.'

'She looks like she might be seventeen, eighteen,' Baker remarked.

'What about time of death?' Craig asked.

'Roughly, I'd say eight to ten hours,' Annie said.

Craig had an idea then. He called Mackay on the phone, asked him a question and waited for him to come over. He did, a few minutes later, holding a plastic bag containing the item Craig had asked about.

'Here we are,' Mackay said, 'an old-lady wristwatch.'

Craig held it up for the others to see. He turned it towards his own face and looked at the face through the plastic. Then he looked at Annie. 'You were right. The time of her death was exactly eleven fifty-seven last night.'

'How do you know?' Annie asked.

'Our killer would take an old wristwatch and put it on each victim's wrist, setting it to the exact time of death. It was his signature, something we didn't put in the papers.'

'Most young girls wear some kind of smart watch nowadays,' Dan said. 'I think pretty much everybody does.'

'Twenty years ago, smart watches weren't around,' Craig said. 'But even if the victim here was wearing one, he would have taken it off, maybe keeping it for a trophy. Then he put the old, unwound watch on her wrist.'

'Maybe he left DNA behind,' Mackay said.

'He was meticulous before. You won't find anything on it.'

'If this is his signature, known only to the police, then there's a good chance that this is the original killer,' Baker said.

'Did you find anything else on her? In her pockets?' Craig asked.

'No, her pockets were empty,' Mackay said. 'Was there something in particular you were looking for?'

'A tarot card. Our killer left a tarot card with each victim.'

'Sorry. There was nothing in her pockets.'

'No matter. I'm still leaning towards this being the original killer rather than a copycat because of the watch,' Craig said. 'But why has he come to Scotland?'

'What's that cut on her forehead?' Baker asked. 'The symbol.'

'I was just getting to that.' Craig was looking at the marking on the girl's forehead, staring at it, unable to take his eyes off it for a moment.

'It's like one of those pentagrams,' Dan said. 'Could this be some ritualistic thing?'

'It's not a pentagram, or a Star of David,' Craig said.

'How do you know?' Baker asked.

Craig looked at him. 'Because I've seen it before.' He paused for a second. 'And there's going to be another victim.'

THREE

The State Hospital was outside the small village of Carnwath, a peaceful little village that just happened to have psychopathic killers for neighbours.

Eve Craig waited in the reception centre building, having left her belongings in a locker. She was scared, nervous, but she was also happy that she was going to see her little boy.

She went through the airport-style security and was then escorted to the family centre. The room had some tables and chairs and a couple of armchairs, but it had an almost disinfectant smell, like everything had been wiped down before she got there.

Her son, Joe, was brought in by two orderlies, followed by one of the psychiatrists.

'Have a seat, Joe,' said the psychiatrist, Christopher Ward. He wore a close-cropped beard, contact lenses rather than glasses (as he'd explained to Eve the last time she was here, as if he had been reading the rule book before he first met her). Ward was skinny, his trousers baggy on him. He dressed like somebody much older than he appeared to be, which was in his mid-thirties.

'Hello, Joe,' Eve said, looking into her son's eyes. There was a slight glaze there, chemically induced. They'd warned her that they would be giving him a 'little something' to take the edge off. Keep his reactions a little bit slow. Just in case.

Joe looked at her and nodded, and there was a light in his eyes, like he was struggling to remember who she was; then it came to him.

'Hello, Mum.'

'Why don't you sit down, Joe?' Ward said.

Joe looked at him as if he'd only just realised the doctor was there. Then he sat down on a chair across from his mother. They were at a table; Ward had told Eve on the phone the day before that Joe wasn't at the armchair stage yet. Better to have an island between them, give the orderlies a fighting chance if things kicked off.

'How have you been?' Eve asked, trying to maintain her composure. She'd promised herself that she wouldn't cry, and Ward had told her that it would be best for Joe if she didn't. He might not realise that she was crying and would get confused, thinking there was something wrong with her.

'I've been fine,' Joe said. 'But that fucking doctor smells.' He had leant forward and said it in a low voice, as if Ward couldn't hear him.

Eve was stuck for words, opening her mouth a couple of times, but nothing came out.

'Why don't you tell your mother what you were up to this week?' Ward said, letting the jibe wash over him.

'I drew some pictures. With crayons. I like drawing. I can draw you something if you like. I'll draw something later.'

'That would be nice, Joe. Can you draw me a dog? Like Finn?'

Joe stared right through her. Then he made eye contact.

'Finn. The big dog. I like him. Can I come home and play with him?'

'Not yet, sweetheart. You have to get better first.'

'Am I ill?' He looked between her and Ward.

Ward smiled at him. 'You've been a little unwell, Joe. You're here so we can help you get better.'

'Oh, right.' Joe looked right at Eve again. 'I'm feeling tired. I'd like to go for a nap now.' He slowly stood up and looked at Ward, who nodded to the orderlies. They both stepped forward and one of them gently guided Joe by the arm.

He left the room without looking back.

Eve sat, tears running down her face, and watched until Joe was out of the room and the door closed. She wasn't aware that Ward had sat down opposite her.

'He's making good progress, Eve. We keep him medicated for the moment. A bit like having a stooky on a broken arm while the bone heals underneath.'

She looked at him now, wiping the tears away with her hands. 'Is he ever going to get back to normal? Like he used to be?'

Ward nodded. 'I think over time, he'll get there. As we talked about before, Joe was an angry teenager, and then when that other influence came into his life, it fed the fire and he turned in a different direction. It wasn't all his fault. He was used and manipulated. But there's a chance we can reverse that, with the proper counselling.'

'He won't go to prison, will he?' It was a question that was full of panic.

'No, I don't think he will. The ultimate decision will be made by the Crown Office, but they'll get a full report from me recommending that Joe walk free when he's completed all the tests and has made progress through me. He might be released under supervision at first, and on medication, but he could live a normal life eventually. But please bear in mind that this isn't going to be an overnight thing. Joe will be with us for a while yet.'

'I understand, Dr Ward.'

'But as you saw, he's making good progress already.'

She nodded and wondered how long her son would have to go about looking like a zombie before he could be released into society again.

For as long as it took for him to show no signs of wanting to kill people with a hammer, she supposed.

FOUR

The victim was seventeen-year-old Andrea Moss, from Kirkcaldy.

'Her prints are in the system,' Craig told the other detectives who were sitting at their desks in the incident room. 'She was part of a demonstration and threw a bottle at one of our officers.'

'Did she do prison time?' Dan asked.

Craig shook his head. 'She got a paltry fine. But she also got a criminal record. We're tracing her next of kin now. Officers are going to the address, doing the death notice.'

'You said at the crime scene there was going to be another victim and you would explain when we got back here,' Dan said.

Craig nodded. 'I'm getting to that.' He stared off

into space for a few moments before looking at them in turn. 'I'd been in CID for about five years when the first murder occurred. It was around Guy Fawkes Night, in North London...'

Starman – back then

'Fucking kids with their explosives,' grumbled DCI Len Turner, coming into the incident room and taking his raincoat off and shaking the rain off it. 'Nearly 'ad me fucking eye out. Little bastards.' He looked at the others, who were sitting at their desks.

'And that was just your own kids,' DS James Craig said.

The room erupted in laughter.

Turner grinned. 'You've been working 'ere too long, son.' He pointed at Craig, then hung his coat on the rack. He looked at the clock and saw they had less than an hour before they were going to leave for the day.

London was under a heavy downpour, which was literally dampening the bonfires that were set up waiting to be torched that night – kids celebrating a man who had tried to blow up the Houses of Parliament hundreds of years ago, and who they didn't give a shit about that but took it as an excuse to set fire to huge piles of wood and set off fireworks, throwing them at old women and bus drivers.

'It's only once a year, boss,' another man said. DI Gerry 'Smithy' Smith was older and carried more weight; he looked like he was heading for an inevitable heart attack.

'Oh, don't start all that shite, Ger. Why do we even celebrate this crap anyway? I wish 'e was around these days, let me tell you. That would sort out those ponces in Parliament, make no mistake.'

'We could just vote them out, sir,' DC Lucy West said.

'If only it were that simple, my girl. Bloody voting's rigged, and we all know it, but nobody does nothing about it. Don't get me started.'

And nobody did. They were going through the day's events when Turner's office phone rang.

'That can't be good news,' Smithy said. He looked at the others. 'Show of hands for the guvnor ignoring the phone?'

They all shot their hands up, including Turner. 'Ah, fuck it. If it's me missus, she'll just nip my fuckin' head when I get in.'

'Surely she'd call you on your mobile, sir?' Craig said.

Turner pointed at him. 'Good call, my son. Must be some fucker upstairs trying to ruin me supper.' The phone stopped ringing. He looked at his watch. Ten minutes to go. He looked at Lucy.

'Do us a favour, Lucy, stand by the window at the door and give us a shout if you see somebody coming.'

Lucy nodded and got up from her desk and stood by the door.

'It's probably going to be some pen-pusher looking to see how much we're spending in the canteen or something. But he's shit out of luck. Five o'clock comes, I'm off.' Turner turned to Lucy. 'All clear?'

She looked at him. 'It is.'

'Right,' Turner said, 'everybody get your jackets on. Lucy, you're the last one, but we'll wait for you.'

They put their jackets on and stood around talking about football until it was five minutes to five.

'Right, Lucy, get your jacket on. Let's get the fuck out of here.'

'Oh shit,' Lucy said, ducking away from the window in the door like somebody had just pointed a gun at her. 'It's Rabbit.'

'Fuck!' Turner said in a raised whisper. 'Get your jackets off, quick. Jimmy, up to the whiteboard.'

Craig whipped his overcoat off in one swift movement, landing it on the back of a chair more through luck than expertise, and he stood at the whiteboard where photos and papers were taped.

The others were back in their chairs as if they'd never left. Turner stood looking at Craig and the board as the incident room door burst open and Detective Superintendent Roger came in like he was looking for the culprit who'd just nicked the last chocolate Hobnob.

'Afternoon, sir. We were just wrapping up the day's events.'

'Never mind that, Turner, we've got some bigger fish to fry. I tried calling you. Don't you answer the phone, man?'

DSup Roger – Rabbit to those who didn't like him, which was pretty much everybody in the station – was in his fifties and overweight, cradling a heart attack, getting ready to let it go. Meantime, he just set his cheeks on fire and poured water over his bald head, simulating his rushing about like a madman. Roger wasn't exactly known for getting off his arse and moving, so for him to grace them with his presence was a rare honour. He was huffing and puffing and if there had been three little piggies in the room, they would have been shiting themselves.

'The phone, sir?' Turner said, looking at Roger like he was daft. After almost thirty years of marriage, he was well practised in the art of lying. Little white ones or the real McCoy, it all came naturally to him. 'The phone didn't ring in here.' He looked at the others. 'Did anybody else hear the phone ring?'

'Not in here,' Smithy said, just as versed in the art of subterfuge and misdirection as Turner.

Craig shook his head. 'Not in here, sir.'

They all knew Turner would take a bullet for each and every one of them, and they treated Turner like a king in return.

'Aw, fuck me, I could have sworn I dialled the right number,' Roger said, looking at a bare patch of the wall like he was mentally scrabbling to think whose number he had actually called.

'It doesn't matter, sir,' Turner added, keeping a straight face, something else he was good at. He practised it when he entered his darkened bedroom at two o'clock in the morning like a commando, which was usually how he made it to bed, crawling along the floor, just before his wife asked him what he was doing. By that time, Turner was so pished he could hardly talk, so he always gave her a quick, 'Shhh, go black to sheep.' He wouldn't remember talking about a black sheep in the morning.

'Anyway, I'm glad I caught you before you all headed off home and had to come back in.'

'What's up, sir?'

'A young girl, found dead. In the middle of a bonfire. Thank Christ it hadn't been lit, but it wasn't for want of trying. Somebody was about to start the festivities early when they saw a foot sticking out.'

Turner let his eyes swiftly divert to the clock on the wall. Two minutes to go. But as old Roger the dodger said, they would have got called back in. Not Turner personally; in his own time he switched his work phone off and used the other one, which was in his wife's name. She'd suggested they both get one and that way they could have some peace, and he'd readily agreed. For occasions like this.

'Right, let's get going. Boys and girls, get your coats' – he almost said *back* – 'on. DSup Roger can fill us in on the way over.'

'Oh no, you're the lead on this, Turner. I have a meeting at five thirty.' Roger handed Turner a slip of paper with an address on it. 'Give me a report in the morning.' With that, he turned on his heel and walked out.

'Fat bastard,' Turner said when he was sure the older man would be out of earshot. 'He's probably got a meeting with the Extreme Doughnut Eating Club.'

The others were getting their coats on, albeit with less enthusiasm than just a few minutes ago.

'Look on the bright side,' Smithy said, 'young Jimmy there said he was taking us out for a couple of swift ones later. It's on him, he said.' He grinned at Craig.

'Is this true?' Turner said to Craig. 'Are we going to get a peek behind the curtains? Get to see the rare species called the Scotsman in its own habitat, the boozer?'

'I'm sure I could stretch to one or two,' Craig said.

'Any more enthusiasm and you'll be giving yourself palpitations,' Turner said. He grinned. 'But good lad. I suspect Lucy might want to break open her piggy bank too.'

'I don't think so,' Lucy answered. 'I kept my mouth shut in front of Roger.'

'So did I,' Craig said.

'Whose arse do you all look at when we're leaving the room?' Lucy asked.

Smithy was the only one who had the decency to pull a beamer.

'Er, well, let's get going, eh?' Turner said, walking to the incident room door, hoping nobody was looking at *his* arse.

They took two cars to the bonfire scene. As Smithy drove, DCI Turner thought his old grandad might have been shiting himself now with all the bangs and explosions. The poor old sod was long gone now, but he had fought bravely during the war. He was in the catering corps, but still, he had done his bit. Made a fair bit of money nicking stuff too, Turner's mum had told him when he was a lad. She said she'd told him that story to teach him that he shouldn't be doing stuff like that, but there was a hint of pride in her voice at the thought of her father procuring some chocolate and nylons off the Yanks in exchange for some of the good meat he'd pilfered.

Turner had wondered what his grandad's own troops thought about eating crap while the Americans gobbled down their ham and potatoes.

'We're here,' Smithy said, skidding the car into

the side of the road like he was re-enacting a scene from an episode of *The Sweeney*.

'Thanks for that, Captain. I was going to say, maybe it would have been quicker if you'd just beamed us up, but not the way you fucking drive.' Turner could have sworn he'd looked over at Smithy a couple of times and seen his eyes rolling about in his head, but he couldn't swear to it.

He let himself out into the cold, dark evening and was disappointed to see the rain had stopped. He held on to the side of the car for a second, letting all of his body parts rearrange themselves back into their original positions. He thought for a second that his arse had eaten the passenger seat, but a quick glance showed it was still intact.

There was a crowd of gawkers looking at the uniforms, who had done a good job of keeping them away from what could easily have been a funeral pyre. A forensics tent had been erected next to where the victim had been found.

The tall pile of wood and other things that could be set alight, like a couple of mattresses and a couch that somebody may or may not be looking for in the morning, was arranged in the shape of a pyramid. It was under one such mattress that the girl had been hidden.

The bonfire sat on a piece of waste ground where a tower block had once sat. Now, tall grass had taken it over. On the other side of the road, the brothers and sisters of the now-departed building were still clinging on to life.

There were a lot of men standing on the periphery of the bonfire, which rose at least fifteen feet into the air: firefighters and men in hard hats, some of them construction workers who had been drafted in with heavy machinery, ready to grab the wood and move it out the way should it come down in an avalanche. Experts had looked at the pile, assessing whether it would be wise to take the whole thing down, but forensics had argued that the crime scene around the victim had to be preserved, so it had been agreed that most of the top half would come down until it was deemed safe for personnel to enter.

They bashed on, the roar of the diesel engines cutting through the air, their flashing yellow lights in competition with the blue lights from the emergency vehicles.

'It couldn't have been easy getting her here unnoticed,' Craig said, 'I mean, all those houses over there. Anybody could have seen him coming here.'

'He could have had a van,' Turner said, 'and

stopped it on the road there, opened a side door and pulled her out, along with an old, shitey mattress. Nobody would have given a toss round here.'

'There's always little bastards floating about here, fucking around on bikes, terrorising old women,' Smithy said.

'This pile doesn't look like it was built by Thomas Telford, so he could have shoved a few pieces to one side and heaved her in,' Turner answered. 'Poor girl.'

'He could have brought the whole bloody lot down on top of himself,' said the forensics team leader, Michael Devlin, standing with his hands on his hips. He was dressed in a disposable suit. 'My boys have taken photos and video, but obviously there's nothing we could get off that wood and debris. The mattress might yield something, but it looks like something a crack whore wouldn't give house room to. We'll process this girl when we get her out, then Professor Have-a-go can do his thing.'

'You better not let him hear you calling him by his nickname,' Turner said, grinning.

Professor Haverstraw oversaw one of the mortuaries in London, and this girl had died in his area.

'Never mind that old sod. It's about time he retired anyway,' Devlin said. 'I hope Maria takes his place. I wish she was here instead of old grumpy balls.'

'Amen,' Turner said.

Just then, the flap of the tent rustled and the godfather of medicine himself walked in, or rather, hobbled in, leaning on a walking stick.

'I hope you haven't been in here cocking things up again, Devlin,' Professor Haverstraw said. He looked old enough to have been in charge of the medical bay on the Ark. He had a full head of hair, now totally grey, and he regularly chastised young men who had gone bald. It was a sign of virility, he would tell the balding men, suggesting that they might be *Jaffas* if they answered in the negative about having children.

'Define *cocking up*,' Devlin said.

'Oh, you know, putting the corpse in a worse state than when she was put in there, that sort of thing. My job is one of skill and expertise. I don't need you adding to the puzzle by having her skewered by a sharp piece of pallet.'

'We'll leave her there, will we? Let you crawl in there on your hands and knees.'

'Aren't you bringing her out?' Haverstraw said, his eyes going wide. 'I mean, my knees aren't what they used to be.'

'Of course we are, daft old sod. We have to wait until they've made it safe.'

'I thought she was dumped on the outside with a mattress over her?' Haverstraw asked.

'She was,' Turner jumped in. 'And unless you want a giant splinter up your jacksie, I'd listen to him.'

'Deary me,' Haverstraw said, turning his nose up at Turner's language.

In the end, the old man conceded the point, and when the bonfire was deemed safe, the forensics crew moved in, along with Turner, Craig and Smithy.

Tarpaulins were held up by uniforms as they conducted their initial investigation of the corpse.

'What the hell is that?' Craig asked.

Turner looked at the girl's forehead, partly covered by her long hair.

Somebody had carved a symbol in her flesh. A star.

FIVE

NOW

Craig looked around at his team, who had been sitting and listening intently. 'She was sixteen years old. She'd been missing from her foster home for three days. They assumed she'd run away again as she'd already done it twice before. Christy McCall was her name, and she died a horrible death.'

'She was the first, you said,' Isla said.

'Yes.' Craig nodded, his thoughts jumping between then and now, clearly picturing the girl's face. 'We didn't know it then, but she'd sneaked out of her house and met up with a friend and gone to a McDonald's. Several witnesses saw them leaving.

Nobody witnessed the two girls being taken away or going with anybody. We checked the CCTV, and nobody approached them either in the restaurant or outside.'

'Where was the other victim found?' DI Max Hold said.

Craig looked at him. 'In a bus depot the day after we found Christy. Sixteen-year-old Mitzy Fraser. She was in a bus at the back of the depot used as a spare. When the driver went to dress the bus – that means fix the screens – he saw her sitting in a seat, dead.'

'How did the killer get somebody into the depot without being spotted?' Dan asked.

'There was a back door at the very rear of the depot which drivers used to take a shortcut, and by all accounts it was never locked, so we surmised he got in through there.'

'How many victims in total?' Isla asked.

'Six in London, two in Halifax. Nobody knows why he went there. He killed four pairs of girls over a two-year period. All of them had a star symbol carved into their forehead. The second victim we found always had the star carved postmortem.'

'It could have been a copycat in Halifax,' Max said.

Craig looked at him. 'No, it was the original killer. He always left two signatures behind, something that was never released to the press. A tarot card in one of the pockets and an old wristwatch on the wrist of each victim.'

'Did forensics find one on our victim?' Dan asked.

'No,' Craig said. 'Nothing in her pockets.'

'We could be looking at a copycat now, do you reckon?' Max asked.

Craig looked directly at him. 'It could be. Or now, after twenty years, he's decided to come north.'

'Were the girls killed at the same time?' Dan asked.

Craig shook his head. 'The second victim was found the following day. Like he'd dealt with one, then dealt with the other.'

Just then, there was a knock on the incident room door, and a uniformed sergeant poked his head in. 'Sorry to disturb you, sir, but a man and a woman have come in and they say they're the parents of a young girl who they want to report missing. Her name is Andrea Moss, our victim.'

SIX

He was used to the smell now. It had bothered him at first, but needs must. Now it was just part of the furniture. Decay, mould, whatever incurable disease that happened to stop by on its way to wherever the fuck it was going. He ignored the smells as he climbed the stairs and entered the bedroom.

'There you are, lazy bones,' he said to the young woman who was lying on the bed. Still dressed in the same clothes she had been wearing when he had given them a lift.

Norma Baxter's wide open, dead eyes stared at him as he stood above her. 'What's that? Why am I doing this? Oh, you really don't want to know that. But rest assured, I'm going to take care of you.'

He looked into eyes that couldn't see anything

anymore. He sat down on the bed at her side and lifted one cold, dead hand, covering it with his other hand.

'I'm going to take care of you. You'll be going home soon. They're waiting for you. They'll be glad to see you.' He smiled. 'Did you have fun last night? I did. I wish we could do it again, but we can't. You won't be here much longer and I have to move on. It was fun while it lasted, though.'

He put her hand down by her side and stood up. The room was stuffy. 'It's sunny outside. Bit cool, but let me open a window and let some fresh air in.' He walked over to the window and looked out over the fields and to the hills in the distance, which looked green and lush after last night's rainfall.

'I wish we could go for a walk. Would you like that?'

'Yes, I would love that,' she replied.

He spun round, his heart beating faster, and she was standing there, looking at him. 'You're alive,' he said, his voice barely a whisper.

'I'm alive any time you want me to be,' she said.

He slowly walked towards her, holding his arms open, getting closer and closer, until she disappeared. He looked. Norma was still on the bed, very much dead.

He took his knife out and sat back down on the bed beside her. 'Time to get you ready.' He smiled. 'Remember the other night? That was fun, wasn't it?'

He thought back, reliving the events of two nights ago, as the tip of his knife cut into her forehead.

SEVEN

Craig and Dan entered the interrogation room where the couple were sitting at a table each with a cup of tea. Craig introduced himself and Dan as they sat down opposite.

'Mr and Mrs Moss,' Craig said, looking at them both in turn. The father looked to be in his fifties; he had a bald head – whatever had been left round the side had been shaved off. His wife looked to be the same age, with short dyed hair and lines on her face that might have come from looking after a teenage daughter who didn't want to play by the rules.

'We want to report our daughter missing,' Moss said. 'And her friend, Norma Baxter – she lives with us too. We were at the station in Kirkcaldy but they told us to come here.'

'Okay, why don't you start by telling me when you last saw them?' Craig knew there were officers on the way to the Moss's address but they must have missed them.

Moss nodded. 'Two days ago. Wednesday. Evening time. They said they were going to the Links in Burntisland, to go on the fairground rides.'

'And they didn't come home, obviously,' Dan said. He sat with a notebook in front of him, scribbling notes down.

'Correct. Andrea texted to say that they were going to stay overnight with her friend.'

'What's the name of this friend they were going to be staying with?' Craig asked.

Moss sniffed and looked at his wife before answering. 'We don't know. We trusted them both, and assumed that it was a girl they were going to be staying with. I mean, Andrea's going to be eighteen next week.'

No, she's not, Craig thought and felt empathy for the couple, who didn't know that yet but would soon. 'How long has Norma lived with you?'

'Her dad died about five years ago, in a car accident, and she got a big payout. Not huge, but enough to start a life when she's an adult. Her mother got left money too, but she died of a stroke a couple of years ago. So we took Norma in then. Andrea asked us to, and we couldn't see her not have a place to live.'

'How do you know the girls are missing?' Dan asked.

'Yesterday, Thursday, we were expecting them home. Not at an exact time, but sometime. They never appeared. I texted Andrea, and she sent a text back. Here. Look at it.'

Moss played around with his phone and then handed it over to Craig, who read the message.

Don't worry, Dad, we're just hanging out. Talk to you later.

'It looks like she's trying to reassure you,' Craig said, handing the phone back.

'You would think. But that's not how Andrea talks in a text. She shortens words with symbols and stuff. Like she's talking another language. Sometimes I have to read it more than once just to know what she's gibbering about. Like, instead of writing *l-a-t-e-r*, she would write *l-8-r*. Stuff like that. So I don't think Andrea has her phone on her. I think somebody has it.'

Craig looked at Dan before looking at Moss, and the other man could tell something was up.

'What is it? What's wrong?'

'I'm sorry to tell you this, Mr and Mrs Moss…'

EIGHT

Craig sat back in his office chair, feeling wiped. Starman. Jesus, it had been a long time since he'd heard that name. All that work hunting the bastard down twenty years ago, yet nothing to show for it. In his experience, copycats came out of the woodwork wanting to put their own mark on the world, but there was always something they did differently that set them apart from the original killer, something they didn't know about.

Not this time. The watch was a dead giveaway. This was the real deal. He was about to lift his phone when his mobile phone rang.

'It's your favourite pathologist,' the caller said.

'Finbar O'Toole? I have to admit, your voice seems to have changed,' Craig said.

'You think you're so funny,' Annie Keller said.

'I do actually. But what can I do for my second favourite pathologist?'

'You're going to hurt for saying that. However, I have a request: can you come along to the post-mortem of Andrea Moss?'

'I can. I have to make a couple of calls first, but I can be down in say –' he looked at his watch – 'an hour. Maybe a little over.'

'Perfect. See you then.'

He hung up and dialled a number on the landline. 'Harry? How you doing, my friend? Jim Craig here.'

DCI Harry McNeil was based in Edinburgh and had met Craig a few times. 'Jim! Good to hear from you, pal. How's things over in the Kingdom?'

'Things are great, but I need your help with something.'

'Fire away.'

'I work with a pathologist over here who's being stalked, and she's starting to get worried.'

'Oh shite. Not one of those weirdo bastards.'

'I'm afraid so. She doesn't have any idea who it is, but her divorce was contentious. She's not sure if he's being a silly bugger or not.'

'I'm assuming he's based over here now?' Harry said.

'Correct. He's a surgeon at the Royal. He's a real player apparently, and now he's seeing a younger woman, a nurse he works with. That's all the intel I have.'

'You want us to check him out?'

'That would be great, if you could.'

'I'll call Finbar O'Toole, one of our pathologists. He's at the hospital often. I'll see if he knows the guy. What's his name?'

'Montgomery Price.'

'I can do that no problem, Jim.'

'Thanks, Harry. Catch up soon for a pint?'

'Absolutely. Maybe we could make a foursome one night and have a meal with the wives.'

'I'd like that.'

'Brilliant. I'll research this guy and get back to you as soon as.'

'Cheers, Harry.'

Craig hung up and dialled another number.

'Barry? It's Jimmy Craig.' DSup Barry Norman still worked for London's Met, but since Craig had left for Scotland, his old boss had told him to use first names.

'Jimmy! How's it going?' The man still had a

thick Glasgow accent.

'To be honest, shite.'

Norman laughed. 'Isn't it always? My wife said I should have got an office job, but what does she know? We don't think we've had a good week if we haven't had a shite day.'

'Exactly.' Craig knew that Norman's wife had left him a long time ago. When he had stayed over at Norman's house on the day of Sharon Bolton's funeral, he had confessed that Deirdre had left him a long time ago.

'So, what can I do you for?'

'You remember the Starman case from twenty years ago?'

'I do. I didn't work the case, but you did. You never got that bastard, if I remember correctly.'

'You do remember correctly. But this is the thing: he's up here now.'

There was silence for a few seconds, and Craig was about to ask the older man if he was still there when Norman answered.

'Scotland? He's up there? After all this time? What the fuck, Jimmy?'

'That's exactly how I felt this morning.'

'Two victims?'

'Not yet, but I expect there to be.'

Norman took in a deep breath before speaking again. 'You know what I'm going to ask you now, don't you?'

'It's not a copycat. There's a detail that only we and the killer would know: the old wristwatch.'

'Fuck. Why now? After twenty years? You think he was in prison?'

'Could be, Barry,' Craig said. 'It's going to take some time to go through the prison service both up here and down there.'

'Especially since the bastard operated in Halifax too.'

'We thought he might have had family there and decided to strike while he was up there for a visit,' Craig said. 'Nothing panned out.'

'I'll get somebody to check on recent releases, but what if he was released a while back and decided to lie low for a while to try and throw us off?' Norman said.

'That's a possibility. It won't do any harm for somebody to check anyway.'

'I'll get right on it, Jimmy.'

'I appreciate it.' Craig paused for a second. 'Have you heard from Sharon Bolton's parents?'

DS Sharon Bolton had been on Craig's team in London, and she'd been murdered by a serial killer who, it turned out, Craig knew but had no idea was a killer.

'Not since the funeral last December. How about you?'

Craig felt the room suddenly get stuffy and loosened his tie before answering. 'I have. I get a letter about once a month.'

'Really? Does he talk about his daughter?'

'In a manner of speaking. He sends me death threats. He talks about how Sharon was too good for the force and if she hadn't joined, then she wouldn't have met me and she would still be alive.'

'The bastard. I'll have somebody go and knock on his fucking door.'

'No, no, Barry, don't do that. He's venting, that's all. He talks about how good Steve Carver and Ronnie Harper are. Better coppers than I ever was.'

DS Ronnie Harper didn't work in Craig's MIT but another one, and Carver was his boss. Harper had shouted abuse at Craig at Sharon's funeral, but Craig had ignored it, seeing that Harper was obviously under the influence of drink.

'Carver took early retirement. He said that the force was fucked when a young DS like Sharon could be targeted. He was very bitter,' Norman said. 'Not with you, but with life in general. He was going to buy a place in Spain, I heard through the grapevine.'

'Sharon's father said that young Ronnie Harper was ill. He blames me for that too.'

'Harper is ill, Jimmy. He had a mental breakdown. They found him wandering about the cemetery where Sharon's buried. He didn't know what day it was, so he was admitted to a psych ward and he's a basket case now. I've never seen anybody react to a death like that before. But he was attached at the hip with Sharon. Loved her more than anything. The doctors said he couldn't take living without her and they reckon he was about to top himself before the patrol turned up at the cemetery. He was moved to an assisted-living facility that specialises in looking after people with mental health problems. He's a wreck, by all accounts. I haven't been in to see him, since he isn't one of my team, but I know others who have, and apparently he sits in a chair drooling all day. They have to keep him drugged up, that's what I heard. He's a shell of his former self.'

'Christ, poor bastard. Sounds like he would take his own life if they took him off the meds,' Craig said.

'That's the way I heard it. He's so young too and had a bright future in front of him. So MIT lost two good men, but they've recruited replacements.

Harper won't be back for a while, if ever. Even if he does come back to work, his days in MIT are finished.'

'I hadn't met him, but Sharon talked highly of him.'

'He's a good guy, except for losing it at the funeral.'

'Stress, Barry. It affects us all in different ways.'

'I know, you're right. Obviously, the stress got to him. That's why he's in the care home.'

'Listen, do you have the number for our friend, the American pathologist who worked on the Starman victims? Christ, what was his name again?'

'Oh, Lance, you mean? Lance Harrison?'

'Aye, that's him. I don't have the number for the mortuary to hand. Do you have it?'

'Well, I haven't heard from Lance since he retired five years ago. I could call the mortuary and see if they can ask him to give you a call. They might not give out his number. Privacy and all that.'

'Brilliant. I just wanted to have a chat with him, see if he has any pointers.'

'I'll get back to you.'

'Thanks, Barry. Talk to you soon.'

Craig hung up and left his office. 'Isla?'

Isla McGregor looked over at him. 'Sir?'

'How did the interview go with the cemetery caretaker?'

'He and his wife were both shocked. Their dog is old, so it didn't pick up anything going on outside last night. They're both in their sixties, and the caretaker is about to retire soon.'

'Good. You don't think they were involved?'

Isla shook her head. 'I don't think so, but we're running their backgrounds right now. I would say somebody just drove in and dumped the girl.'

'Okay. Grab your jacket; we're going to Dunfermline.'

She got up and followed him out of the incident room. Detective Chief Superintendent Bill Walker was walking along the corridor towards them.

'Jimmy! Just the man I wanted to talk to.'

'Afternoon, sir,' Craig said.

'I've been talking to my counterpart down in Halifax, England. He's sending two men up here to go over the Starman case with you, since they had the killer on their patch as well, twenty years ago.'

'Are they coming today?' Craig asked.

'Yes. I gave the DCI your number. Tom Bailey's his name. Expect him to make contact with you.'

'A Yorkshireman?'

'Through and through, apparently. Let him join the investigation, but don't let him take over it.'

'As if.'

'Right, carry on, Jimmy. Keep me in the loop regarding this case. I can't believe this bastard is up here now. Mark Baker filled me in earlier.'

'Hopefully, this time we'll catch him.'

'I hope so, Jimmy. I hope so.'

NINE

Raymond Taylor talked to the dead. He didn't see them or anything like that. He just talked to them, and out loud too, if they were alone. Like he was with this young female he was pushing on the gurney. He took her into the freight lift and pushed the button for the mortuary.

'I can't believe this, Suzie. Did you have one wee drink too many? I can understand that you like to go out and have a good time, but you should have been more careful.' He smiled at her. He rolled the sheet back so he could see her face more clearly. She was blonde, with beautiful green eyes that she would never be able to see with again.

'Oh, Raymond, don't lecture me. It was just a few tequila shots. I was out with the girls and you know how that goes. Plus, we couldn't find a taxi, so I drove home. Have you ever driven buzzed?'

He stared into her eyes. 'Buzzed, Suzie? You were more than buzzed, from what I heard. But I don't blame you. If I was your husband, I would have stayed sober and come and driven you home. How long have you been married?'

'Six months.'

'He's a loser, you know that? Six months? I wouldn't have let you out of my sight. Well, you know what I mean. I'd have let you go out with your pals, of course, but I would have been waiting at home for you. Not like that loser, Ryan.'

'I love Ryan. He's so sweet to me.'

'Look, I didn't want to say this, but when they switched off your machines, your sister leaned into him and started crying, and he was holding on a little too tight if you ask me.'

'What are you trying to say?'

'I think he has designs on your sister.'

'Ryan? No. He wouldn't do that. And my sister wouldn't encourage it.'

'I'm just saying what I was seeing,' Raymond said.

'Huh. What a lousy bastard.'

'I know, right? But let me run this by you: how

about you and I leave here and go have a drink somewhere quiet? Somewhere classy? On me. I'll buy you anything you want.'

'I'd love that. I think you're right about Ryan. There were signs, but I overlooked them. He was working late all the time, but coming home with drink on his breath.'

'There you go, sweetheart. I'll treat you like a princess. Divorce him, and I'll take care of you for the rest of your life.'

'I think I'm falling in love with you, Raymond.'

'I'm falling in love with you too, Suzie. I knew I was the minute I clapped eyes on you. You know something?' Raymond asked.

'What?'

'If it was me, I'd have kept you on life support. But between you and me, I don't think they care about people. They need the beds, so they take you off life support so you'll die. And don't get me started on harvesting organs. Nope. I won't go there. They forget I see and hear things on the wards. Hear them talking. I'm invisible, though. I'm a porter, so I glide about this hospital without anybody ever seeing me. I'm a ghost. I was there – I saw what happened. I think Ryan was too quick to make the decision to switch you off, but of course the doctor piped up, saying, "It's not your decision, it's mine." Of course he's going to say that. It takes the burden off the family member and edges them towards the decision the doctor wants. I think when Ryan had your sister in his arms, that decision was made a whole lot easier.'

He grinned and ran a hand through her hair. 'I have to take you in here now, but we'll talk later,' Raymond said, pulling the cover back over her face as the lift stopped at mortuary level.

His imagined life with a woman he didn't know when she was alive. It made him happy to think she might have run away with him. If only he could find a woman with a pulse to run away with him.

He wheeled the young woman into the refrigerated area, where she would be kept until it was time for the postmortem.

He slid her into one of the drawers, smiled, closed the door and pulled the gurney back. Suzie would have been far better off with him rather than that lousy bastard of a husband. Ryan was spilling crocodile tears now, but give him five minutes and he'd be shagging Suzie's sister.

'Oh, what could have been, sweetheart. Another time, another place.'

Raymond pushed the gurney along the corridor

and stopped at Annie Keller's office. He went inside and laid the paperwork for Suzie on her desk.

He looked around. The mortuary assistants were out doing God knows what and the place was deadly quiet. He sat down on Annie's office chair and started looking in her drawers, seeing if she had any packets of biscuits lying around, but he couldn't see any. Shame. He was peckish now.

He looked at the certificates on the wall. He liked Annie. She was good-looking, smart, had a sharp wit. He wanted to ask her out but had yet to pluck up the courage. Would she go out with him, a lowly porter? Why not? He wasn't exactly the best-looking guy in the hospital, but neither did he look like his face had gone through a mincer. He would bide his time and then casually strike up a conversation and how could she resist his charm? Suzie thought he was charming. Hell, she would have left her husband for him.

Raymond was in between Suzie's age and Annie's age: thirty-seven. The prime of his life. Even his mother said so.

He wasn't going to be a porter all of his life. Maybe he was too old to be a doctor, but he could certainly become a writer like he'd always wanted to. He wrote in his bedroom on a laptop he'd bought off one of the other lads at work. It was an old thing, but all he needed it for was to put his words down on paper. Or the screen.

He'd always been a writer. That was what he read online: if you write, you're a writer, no matter what anybody else says. He never spoke about it, especially to his mother. She probably thought he was visiting the dark web, talking to girls who would cut your throat if you turned your back on them, but he wasn't interested in that. He was interested in a land that only existed in his mind.

He wrote fantasy books, and had completed several, but had never found the nerve to post them off to one of those highfalutin agents in London. Then he had spoken to a writer one day as he pushed her in a wheelchair. She'd been in to have a toenail removed and he had made sure she got to the front door without falling over. They got talking about writing after he discovered she was a writer. She was self-publishing online and her sales were getting better. She recommended he try it. By all accounts, it was easy.

His fictitious world was called –

'What are you doing in here?'

The voice made him jump. He hadn't realised he

had put his feet up on Annie Keller's desk and sat back with his hands behind his head.

He stared at her, wide-eyed. He had only briefly spoken to her before, and in very short sentences. It was like when you were interested in a woman at a club and you wanted to ask her to dance, and you finally plucked up the courage and went across, but before you could even ask her to dance, her response was, 'Piss off.'

He smiled at her, maybe not his best smile, but one that didn't make him look demented. 'Sorry. I just took the weight off for a second. I've been on my feet all day.'

'What's going on?' Raymond heard another voice and looked out the window into the corridor. He saw a man, one of the mortuary assistants, and a woman, some stuck-up snot from one of the labs upstairs.

The man was Davie Cook. A bit older than Raymond, and he had one of those fancy goatee beards, which Raymond thought was fitting, because the bastard looked like a fucking goat. He would never say that to the man's face, of course, because from what he'd heard, Cook used to play rugby, and he could probably balance a rugby ball on his knob.

'I was just taking a pew for a minute. I twisted my knee the other day and it's giving me some pain.

Nothing serious, but I thought I'd take the opportunity to rest it for a couple of minutes.'

'In Dr Keller's office?' Cook made it sound like Raymond had been sitting there with his trousers round his ankles.

'Just for a couple of minutes, Davie.' He slowly stood up, pretend-wincing at the injury he'd just made up. 'Apologies, Doctor. It'll never happen again. I brought a deceased person down and left the paperwork in your tray. I overstepped the line. Please accept my apologies.'

'It's not that big a deal. I was just startled, that's all.' Annie stepped aside for him as he left the office.

'Thank you for understanding,' Raymond said when he was in the corridor and safely out of Cook's reach should the other man decide to take a swing. He walked away, putting on a little limp in case the bastard was watching.

At the lift, he pressed the button and waited for the doors to open. When they did, a man in a suit stepped out with a young woman in tow. Raymond smiled at her, but as usual they both looked right through him. Maybe he really was a ghost after all.

'Goodbye, Suzie,' he said as the doors slid closed. 'Safe travels.'

TEN

DCI Tom Bailey was looking forward to the weekend, which was only a day away. Saturday was holding out its hand for him, telling him to grab hold and come in, the water was warm. Dip his toes, see what was in store for him.

Normally, the weekend promised a night out with the boys on Friday in Halifax city centre, with the obligatory hangover on Saturday morning, followed by the hair of the dog in his local in the afternoon and then a night out with his wife.

This week had been a real bastard, but in his line of work, it went with the territory. Some bastard had made a complaint against him for being too rough. A lousy little sheep shagger called Lewis Cairns who had been selling little bags of what he promised would be 'cloud nine' but had actually turned out to be bags of the back-door trots. He'd been mixing the good stuff with laxative again.

Bailey had happened to slip when they were arresting Cairns and his boot had connected with the man's wedding tackle.

Now, Bailey was sitting in his boss's office instead of being in the incident room.

'You know what these fooking dirtbags are like, boss,' he said, trying to keep the irritation out of his voice.

Detective Superintendent Wallace Campbell took his glasses off and laid them on his desk in front of him. 'Aye, I do know what these wee bawbags are like, but this one has a lawyer now, and that same lawyer has promised a lawsuit, because Cairns is getting married soon and he's worried that he won't be able to provide his new bride with some offspring.'

The Scotsman sat back in his chair and rubbed the bridge of his nose, which had been broken on more than one occasion. Campbell was a big man, broad-shouldered, but he paled in comparison to Bailey's six foot six. If anybody was considering building a brick shithouse from scratch, they could do worse than model it on Tom Bailey, who was built like one.

'If that's the case, then I did the world a favour,' Bailey said.

'That's not the point, Tom.'

'I know, but the little fooker was fighting us, and I slipped in the struggle and my foot connected wi' his nether regions.' His Yorkshire accent was thick, and if ever a recording were made of his and Campbell's accents and sent into outer space on a disc, and some alien race were to find it, they'd scratch their heads and ask, *What the fuck is this?* Then they'd turn around and head back to where they came from.

'That's what we'll stick with, of course,' Campbell said, on the fence as to whether he believed Bailey's story or not.

'I've got my team who'll back me up. And Mad Bastard McCann from the drugs squad. He was there. He witnessed everything.'

Campbell nodded. McCann was just as daft as Bailey, and no doubt they would back each other up no matter what the other one had done, but he kept this thought to himself.

'Right, leave it with me. It's not the first time I've put my hand down the shitter and pulled you out of it,' Campbell said.

'For which I will be eternally –'

Campbell held up a hand. 'Keep that thought in mind when I give you the next piece of good news.'

'Cairns has decided on a life of celibacy after all?'

'Let's forget that wee shite just now. This is something else entirely. You're going on a trip.'

Bailey's eyebrows shot up. 'Did I win a raffle I don't know I bought a ticket for?'

'If that's the spin you want to put on it,' Campbell said. 'You're going on a trip and it will be far away. You'll be taking a friend with you. You'll be leaving today.'

Maybe the weekend was going to start early after all. 'Is it Spain? With me golfing buddy, Sam?'

'Not quite. This trip doesn't involve Spain, golf or one of your dodgy mates.'

'Sam's not dodgy, boss.'

'I just told you it doesn't involve him anyway, Tom. Pay attention.'

Fook's sake. 'Where is it then?' Bailey was starting to have one of his bad feelings, like when they'd raided a big mansion one night and it had ended up with him throwing somebody out of a first-floor window. Lucky for that bastard, he had landed in a bush. The man had no doubt given a little shout-out to the man upstairs about not calling him home just yet, and his prayers had been answered. The other prayers about not being put away for a long time had fallen on deaf ears after the judge had found out he had stabbed one of Bailey's team.

'My home country, if not my hometown,' Campbell said.

Bailey made direct eye contact with him. 'If you don't mind me saying, boss, could you not talk in riddles?'

'Scotland, Tom, Scotland.'

'I know where you come from. But why would I want to go there?'

'It's not a choice. You don't get to toss a coin and call it in the air. This is from further up the food chain. There's been a murder in Fife, and it bears a striking resemblance to a murder here in Halifax twenty years ago. A young girl had her throat slashed and a marking cut on her forehead. You remember that?'

Bailey nodded. 'Aye. The bastard operated in London too, if I remember correctly.'

'Your memory serves you well. He slashed his victims' throats and then cut a star into the flesh on their foreheads. "Starman" the press dubbed him.'

'God bless the rags and their need to immortalise serial killers.'

'If your memory is serving you as well as you say it is, then you will remember he was never caught.'

Bailey thought the older man was a cheating bastard as he had a sheet of paper in front of him and he was willing to bet it wasn't the lunch menu from the canteen.

'I do remember that. I'd only been in CID a couple of years.' He took his eyes away from the sheet of paper and looked at his boss again. 'Are you trying to tell me we got him after all these years?'

'No, Tom, I'm trying to tell you there's a victim in Fife who's just been murdered in the same way. Copycat? Original killer decided to move north? That's what I want you to go and find out. See what we're dealing with.'

'I don't think the Scots will be best pleased with me trampling about all over their case.'

'Since when did you care about anybody's feelings?' Campbell said.

This was true, but Saturday was knocking on the door, wanting Bailey to come out and play.

'You have a good point there, boss.'

'Good. Go and pack a bag and grab a pool car, and I'll text you the details. The production department will have a hotel sorted for you by the time you get up there.'

'I'm leaving right away, I take it?'

'You're both leaving right away, yes.'

'Both?' The question wasn't asked with any enthusiasm.

'I said you were going with a friend. You and DS Smalls.'

'Biggie's coming?' Bailey's nickname for Michael Smalls, one of his sergeants.

'Yes. Even though you'll be there over the weekend, I want an update every day.'

'I wouldn't want to disturb you at the country club, sir.'

'I don't mind taking a call when it's from you, Tom.'

Bastard.

'I should get home and break the news to my wife that our weekend of wine and debauchery has taken an unexpected turn.'

'Rather you than me.' Campbell had met Bailey's wife, a woman who was not known for taking shite off anybody.

Bailey stood up. 'I'll get off now.'

Campbell nodded. 'You'll have the details of where to go before you leave. Thanks, Tom.'

Bailey nodded, then left the office. Starman. He

was another one who was getting a boot in the bollocks if Bailey got hold of him.

ELEVEN

'Are you okay?' Craig said to Annie as he and Isla reached her office. He saw Annie was wiping down her chair with antiseptic wipes. A man and woman were standing outside, and the male looked at Craig with suspicion.

'She got a fright, that's all,' Davie Cook said, with a face like thunder. 'That porter, Raymond Taylor, was sitting in her office. I told him to beat it.'

'It's okay, Davie. I'm expecting DCI Craig and DS McGregor.'

'I'll take those samples now, Davie,' the young female said to Cook, and they both turned away and left without saying another word.

'That man who just got in the lift was sitting on my chair when I got here. I was startled, that's all.'

'Do you think Taylor could be the stalker?'

'Stalker?' Isla said, her eyes going wide.

'Oh, shite,' Craig said. 'Me and my big mouth.'

'It's okay, Jimmy, I was going to tell Isla tonight anyway. We're going for a drink,' Annie said. She looked at Isla. 'I was going to tell you later.'

'Bloody hell, Annie. A stalker? And you thought it might be a guy who was just sitting in your office? And you came in here on your own, and he could have had a knife or anything.'

'He's a porter here. He brings the deceased down from the wards. He's quiet. I've never really had a conversation with him, just a quick hello in passing. He's harmless.'

'Is he?' Isla said, her voice tinged with anger. 'Don't you do that to me again, Annie Keller. If you're having a problem with anybody, you bloody well tell me. Christ. And you should know better than to keep that from me,' she said to Craig. 'Sir.'

'It wasn't my place to talk about Annie's problem,' Craig said in his own defence. 'Besides, I only found out this morning.'

'It's true, he did,' Annie confirmed, tossing the wipes into her bin and then rubbing her hands with hand sanitiser.

'If we're going out for a drink, I should know these things,' Isla said. 'Just in case.'

'I'm sorry. I was going to tell you. Honest.' Annie's hands were shaking.

Isla went round to her and put her arms around her. 'Tell me what's been going on.' She let her go and Annie repeated what she'd told Craig earlier in the day, about the letters and gifts being sent to her house, then the threatening letters.

'Do you think it's your ex messing about?' Isla said.

'That's what I asked,' Craig said.

'It wouldn't surprise me. He turned into a real prick. He took it badly when I caught him cheating and told him to leave. He was not happy about that. He had nowhere to go and his bit on the side was married so he couldn't go and stay with her. He stayed on his brother's couch for a while before moving to Edinburgh.'

'What about his brother?' Craig asked. 'Do you think he's capable?'

Annie shook her head. 'No. Gerry's a sweetheart. As soon as he learned Monty was shagging around, he told him to leave. Besides, Gerry's in a wheelchair. And he has a girlfriend. I couldn't think of a reason he would do such a thing. He's been on my side since Monty and I divorced. And the three of us, me and Gerry and his girlfriend, have a meal out regularly.'

'What's that porter's name?' Craig asked.

'Raymond...' Annie said, looking at the ceiling for inspiration. 'Raymond...Raymond...It's on the tip of my tongue.'

'That's a funny name for a bloke,' Isla said.

'You're not helping.' Annie looked directly at her. 'Taylor!' She snapped her fingers. 'Mark Baker came into my mind for some reason, and I thought about how he looked like he needed a new suit. Taylor.'

'I'll check him out, see if he's got a record,' Craig said.

'Don't ruffle any feathers, please, Jimmy,' Annie said.

'You won't be saying that if he's a member of an axe-throwing club and he has a collection of them,' Isla said.

'True. Okay, do what you think's best. Thank you both for caring.'

'You're like family,' Isla said. Craig nodded his head in agreement. Like family, but not like a certain member of his own family.

'Right, let's get on with the postmortem,' Annie

said. 'But first, the tox report shows that Andrea Moss had Rohypnol in her system. And plenty of alcohol, so we can assume that her killer doped her first.'

'And we have to assume that he doped her friend too. She hasn't been found yet, but she will be,' Craig said.

'How do you know?'

'He'll want to hide her for now, but he'll also want her to be found when he dumps her.'

'Let me show you something,' Annie said. She reached into a drawer and took out a small polythene bag and held it up for them to see. 'This was hidden in Amanda's underpants.'

It was a tarot card.

TWELVE

'Welcome to Scotland!' DS Michael Smalls shouted.

DCI Tom Bailey jumped awake from the passenger seat, just in time to see the blue-and-white road sign flash by him. 'Ya daft bastard. I was napping there. Fooking shouting out like that.'

They were heading up the A1 from Halifax and had just passed Berwick-upon-Tweed and had now crossed the border.

'Napping?' Biggie said. 'You were snoring so loud, I thought the transmission was fucked.' Biggie was from the south of England originally and was what Bailey called 'a southern wank'.

'I'll give you fooking transmission. Just shut your fooking pie-hole until we get to Edinburgh.' Bailey tutted and shook his head. He couldn't believe the lass in the production department had booked them into a hotel on the outskirts of Edinburgh. Like there were no hotels in fooking Fife. She had said all the good ones were booked up at the last minute so she thought one near the airport would be okay. He had reminded her that they weren't flying up.

Bailey raised his arse off the seat and let out a ripper. 'That'll teach you to fooking wake me up.'

'Smelly bastard,' Biggie said, grinning. He and Bailey had been like best friends since the younger detective had hammered a couple of lads who had just stabbed Bailey twice. Luckily, the older detective hadn't suffered serious injuries, but he might have if Biggie hadn't stepped in and taken care of the bastards.

'Wake me up when we're at the hotel, and not a minute before,' Bailey warned, then reclined his seat even more.

Biggie joined the Edinburgh bypass and followed the satnav all the way to the Gogar roundabout, then found the hotel near the Glasgow railway line. He parked in the car park and turned the engine off.

'Aaarrgh!' he shouted.

'Wha...wha...?' Bailey said, shooting upright. He saw a hedge in front of them and for a moment he thought they were leaving the road, but then he saw Biggie laughing and he realised the engine was off.

'You told me to wake you when we got here,' Biggie said, grinning.

'You fooking little bastard. I nearly shat meself.'

They were at the Premier Inn at Edinburgh Business Park. It looked a decent enough hotel. Once his heart had stopped racing, Bailey got out of the car, while Biggie took the luggage out of the back and stretched his back. In the distance was the bypass they'd just come off. Traffic was building up even this early, in the mid-afternoon, as drivers started to escape the city.

'Right, let's get checked in. I'm bursting for a piss,' Bailey said, grabbing the extending handle of his case, and they started walking to the back entrance of the hotel.

Inside the lobby, there were a few couples standing about, waiting in front of the check-in desk, where a young man was looking at a computer.

'We have two rooms –' Bailey started to say, but the man put up a hand.

'Check-in is at three o'clock.'

Bailey looked at his watch: 2.58.

'It's almost three now.'

'But it's not three, is it?'

'Listen,' Bailey said, taking his warrant card out and showing it to the man, 'we're here on a murder investigation. We've not got time to piss about waiting.'

'You'll just have to. The computers don't open until three.'

'Fook's sake.' Bailey turned to the others. 'You lot don't mind if we jump the queue, do you?'

One older woman was about to open her mouth when her husband nudged her, and she closed it again. The six-foot-six Yorkshireman could go to the front if he wanted to.

'Right then, name?' the receptionist said.

'DCI Bailey. DS Smalls.'

The man tutted and played around on his keyboard, then handed over two keycards. Bailey grabbed them.

'There's a Costa coffee shop right there –' the receptionist started to say.

'I couldn't give a fook,' Bailey said, and he and Biggie headed over to the lifts. Two vending machines sat opposite the lift doors, and Biggie swiped his credit card. 'You want anything, Tom?'

'Aye, go on then. Something wrapped in chocolate. And get us a bottle of that piss water they drink up here.'

'Fat bastard,' Biggie said. 'If Cilla asks me, I'll fucking tell her you were eating shite again.'

'My wife won't believe anything that comes out of your mouth, ya slavering coont.'

Chocolate bars and cans of Irn-Bru dispensed, Bailey swiped his card at the lift call button and the doors slid open. They took the lift to the second floor.

'You're over there,' Bailey said. 'I'm in here.' He nodded to his room door on the opposite side. 'If you get scared through the night, don't be knocking on my fooking door, or I'll boot your bollocks.'

'I was going to say that to you, big fanny.'

Bailey grinned. 'You know you're the only man on this earth who could call me that and walk away?'

'I know. Same goes for you.'

'Stop talking through your arse. Five minutes, back at the lift. Time for a piss, and a quick chocolate bar scran. And brush your teeth; your fooking breath's honking. I'll give this DCI Craig a call, see where the bastard's at.'

Bailey let himself into his room, dumped his case on a chair – not the bed – and looked out of his window. The Glasgow line was on his right, and a train was approaching the station. In the distance, he saw Edinburgh Castle on the horizon. Over to the right of that was Arthur's Seat. He'd come here years ago with his little boy, six months before he died. A memory suddenly rushed into his head and he fought to control his emotions.

Biggie was like a son to Bailey now, and God help any bastard who touched the young man. Cilla loved the young lad too, and regularly had him round for dinner.

He used the bathroom and made sure his eyes didn't look like somebody had blown cigarette smoke into them, then met Biggie at the lift.

THIRTEEN

Craig was sitting drinking coffee with Isla and Annie when Tom Bailey and Michael Smalls walked along the corridor. The big man stopped outside the office and looked in.

'DCI Bailey, looking for DCI Craig.'

Craig stood up from the chair he was sitting in and put his mug of coffee down on Annie's desk. The big man towered over him as he stepped into the office.

'I'm Craig. Call me Jimmy.' He stuck out a hand for Bailey to shake and he noticed how strong the man's grip was.

'Pleased to meet you, Jimmy. Tom. This is my sidekick, DS Mike Smalls.' Bailey turned to look at Biggie. 'Don't just stand there fooking gawping – get in here and shake the man's hand.' He stepped aside to let Biggie in. Craig shook the other man's hand and introduced them both to Isla and Annie.

'Why don't we go to the break room and we can discuss the case,' Annie said.

'Lead the way, lass.'

Annie raised her eyebrows behind Bailey's back. *Lass?* she mouthed at Craig, who just smiled and shrugged his shoulders.

They walked along the corridor, past the lifts and into a room that had two tables and a smattering of mismatched chairs. There was a kettle and Isla switched it on.

'Give the lass a hand, Biggie,' Bailey said to his partner.

Annie, Craig and Bailey sat at the table while the two DSs made the coffees.

'How was your trip?' Craig asked.

'I got a right good fooking nap. Luckily for me, Biggie drives like an old granny going to church on a Sunday.'

'Good. Where are you staying?'

Bailey shook his head. 'The lass who booked us in got us a hotel across the water in Edinburgh Park. Premier Inn. Nice place, but she didn't put too much thought into getting us a place. I told the lad there that there are hotels in Fife, but for some reason we got put in Edinburgh. At least it wasn't in the city centre.'

They made small talk while the coffees were made, then when they were all at the table, Craig brought out the tarot card from his inside pocket, still in the plastic bag.

'Death,' Bailey said, looking at it. The card showed the Grim Reaper holding his scythe. 'The other one is going to be the Devil. If there is another one.'

'There will be,' Craig said. 'I'd bet a month's salary on it.'

'What about a watch?'

Craig nodded. 'There was what our forensics guy called "an old-lady's watch". It was set to what we believe was her time of death. Which was last night. She was found in the early hours of this morning, and my team responded after the forensics team did their thing. We believe that the two young women were taken on Wednesday night after going to the funfair in Burntisland. He took them somewhere and spent time with them before killing them. Assuming there's a second victim, but we know from the parents that a second girl, who lives with them, was out with their daughter and she's missing too.'

'This other girl is going to be the next victim, more than likely.'

'I would say so.'

Bailey turned to Annie. 'This card was found in her pocket?'

Annie shook her head. 'No, it was in her underpants.'

Bailey looked puzzled. 'That's a change in the MO. The victims in Halifax had the cards in their pockets. And from the reports I read, same with the victims in London.'

'That was it exactly,' Craig said.

'I wonder why he changed it?' Bailey said.

'Who knows?' Craig said. He looked at Annie. 'Was there any sexual assault?'

'No. I did an initial exam and there was no sign. But why don't we go and have a look at her before I do the PM tomorrow?'

Craig nodded. 'Let's go through to the fridge area, Tom.'

'Aye, fine.'

They all stood up and left the break room. Annie led the way down the brightly lit corridor to the post-mortem suite, and they went through the rubber doors into the large room. It was much cooler in here, and white and sterile-smelling – Craig noticed Bailey wrinkling his nose.

'I've been in too many of these places over the years,' Bailey said. 'Every one of them smells the same. Like my old granny.'

'You and me both,' Craig said. 'I transferred up from the Met six months ago. The ones that got to me were the poor sods we fished out of the Thames. Put me right off fish, that did.'

'Well, that's me not having fish fingers for dinner tonight,' Annie said.

'More of a caviar and champagne lass, are you?' Bailey said with a grin.

'On what they pay us up here? I seriously doubt it.'

The mortuary assistant, Davie Cook, appeared.

'Davie? You got a minute?' Annie said.

'Of course. I was on my way to sterilise some equipment, but whatever you need,' he said, smiling.

'The detectives here would like to see Andrea Moss, if you could pull her out of the drawer.'

'Absolutely. Excuse me, ladies and gentlemen.' Cook stepped past them and pulled the release handle on one of the drawers, then slid out the steel table with a sheet-covered corpse on it.

Annie stepped forward. The body was at waist

level for most of them. She gently pulled the sheet back, revealing the ashen face of the young woman, not even out of her teens.

Bailey peered closely at the star carved on her forehead. Then he straightened up and looked at Craig. 'You remember your victims down in London?'

'Of course.'

'Have a look at her cut.'

All eyes were on the star carved into her forehead. Craig did what Bailey had just done: peered closer. He stood up straight and looked at Bailey, who in turn looked at Annie.

'Thanks. You can put her back now.'

Cook covered Andrea's face with the sheet before gently sliding her back into the unit and closing the door. 'Anything else, Doctor?'

'No, thanks, Davie.'

'No problem.' He smiled at the detectives before moving off to continue what he was doing before they called him over. Bailey watched the young man leave.

'Can we talk in private?' Bailey said to Craig.

'You can use my office,' Annie said.

The two senior detectives left the suite and headed back along to Annie's office.

'Listen, Jimmy, I don't know about the victims in London, but the two we had in Halifax had the same kind of symbol carved into their heads, but carved deep. Down to the bone.'

'Ours did too, back down south.'

'You noticed that in there, didn't you?'

Craig nodded. Earlier in the day, when the young woman had been sitting leaning against the gravestone, he hadn't noticed because he hadn't got a close-up view of the wound. Now that he had in the mortuary, he'd noticed the difference right away.

'It's more superficial,' he said to Bailey. 'Not deep at all. Which means our killer isn't as strong as he was twenty years ago, or –'

'Or we have a copycat. A very clever one, but a copycat.'

'This is all going to shite. Everything points to the real killer being up here, except for the shallow cut.'

'I just want us to keep an open mind on this,' Bailey said.

'We will, Tom.' Craig sat on the edge of Annie's desk and knew he had to call somebody else from his past.

FOURTEEN

When he got home, Craig sat in one of the chairs in the little nook in the living room. The bedrooms were on the entrance level, with the living room, kitchen and a couple of other rooms on the upper level. This afforded them a view over to the bridges in the distance. The sun was over to the west, getting ready to sign off for the day in a few hours. Meantime, it was still lighting the water.

He looked at the book Annie had given him for Eve. He hadn't had the heart to tell Annie that he and Eve were no longer an item. His wife had decided she wanted to move closer to the State Hospital, and he was welcome to join her, but she had put him in an impossible situation. Now, the only time they talked was when she had gone in to see Joe, which was getting more frequent since she was a teacher and not working for the summer. He didn't know what his wife would do when it was time to go back to school.

He called her.

'Hello, Eve,' he said.

'Oh, hi, Jim.'

'I have a book for you from Annie,' he said. Finn, their German Shepherd, had greeted him at the door downstairs, and now he was sitting next to Craig, getting his head petted.

'Tell her thanks. What one is it?'

Why don't you fucking come home and find out?
'It's a Freida McFadden. I didn't realise you read these types of books. I thought you were all about romance these days?' he said. He'd taken his jacket off and loosened his tie, and he thought about having a glass of wine, but he didn't want to start just now. The dog lay down beside him.

'I was for a while, but now I'm into psychological thrillers.'

Fuck it, he thought, reaching for the bottle, and poured himself a half glass.

'We have a guy up from Halifax –' he started to

say, but Eve interrupted him, all signs of pleasantries now gone.

'Aren't you going to ask about our son? The serial killer.'

'I didn't want to jump all over you with questions,' he said, sipping the wine.

'Ask away now. I've had a few glasses of wine that have taken the edge off.'

'Are you sure you should be doing that? Going in buzzed to see Joe?' He knew this was going to lead to an argument just like the ones they'd had recently.

'I'm not going to be fucking buzzed. I'll be fine in the morning.'

'I'm just trying to save you from yourself.'

'Ah. Saving me. Okay. But at least pretend you fucking care about our son.'

'I do care about him. Christ. We can talk about him without you having to put your head down the toilet afterwards.' He paused, trying to rein it in. 'So how is he?'

'Getting better. Now, I still think he'd be a raging nutball if he was taken off the meds, but that's just a layman's opinion. What the fuck do I know? Hmm? I know that this time last year, I had a son who appeared to be normal. A son who I thought was at university but in all reality was killing people and wasn't even at fucking university anymore. And I fucking hate the other person who's living inside his head!'

Finn sat up, knowing there was something wrong, ready to spring into action.

'Maybe the treatment will help him and we'll be able to have him back home one day,' Craig said. 'That means we need to stay strong for him. Getting pished every night and arguing all the time isn't going to make this a suitable place for him to come back to. If it's deemed he didn't know what he was doing, he'll be released under supervision, and he'll be coming home. That's a long way off, but still, we need to present a united front.'

And we'll have to discuss our living arrangements since you left me.

Eve started crying. 'I know you're right. I'm sorry. For everything. For being a bitch and getting drunk all the time. It won't happen again.'

'It's fine. You've been under a lot of stress recently,' Craig said, feeling bad that he'd raised his voice. 'Will you be coming home soon?'

'You ask me that every day,' Eve said. 'I told you, a separation for a little while will do us both good. I'm staying in this little place down here so I can see Joe every day. I can see him as often as I want, and

I'm taking advantage of that. Now that school's out and I have time on my hands, why not?'

'Why not, Eve?' Craig said, unable to hold back the frustration. 'You have a life up here with me.'

'I thought you said you understood?'

'I did. I do. But I'd like to think my wife would like to come home.'

'Don't pressure me, Jim. I'll be in touch regularly. I told you that if you didn't want to come down here with me, I'd leave on my own, and that's what I did.'

'I have to make a phone call now, Eve.'

'Okay.'

He waited for her to say, 'I love you', but she just hung up. After all these years of being married, that shouldn't have bothered him, but it did. And the way she casually used the word 'separation' bothered him. He hadn't seen her for two months, and he knew that their marriage was dead in the water.

He took another sip of the wine and tried to clear the image of his wife out of his mind and thought about the man he was about to call.

Craig had kept in touch with his boss at the Met after he retired. Ex-DCI Len Turner had retired to the country, preferring country life after living in London all his days. While he was still based in London, Craig had often caught up with Turner in the small village pub, which was only a train ride away for Craig, and they'd chatted on the phone at least once a month, Craig keeping Turner in the loop with current cases.

'Jim!' the older man said, answering his phone. 'How's it up there in the sticks? Doing your head in yet, mate?'

'You asked me that when I called you on Hogmanay.'

'That was six months ago. A man can go crazy in that time, me old son. I've seen it happen.'

'Away and don't talk pish.'

'Swear on my mam's life,' Turner said.

'Your mother's dead, Len.'

Turner laughed. 'That's why you're one of the best detectives I ever worked with.'

'Listen, boss, I wanted to run something past you. On the QT, though.'

'You know it won't go any further, Jimmy.'

'I know; that's why I'm sharing this. Starman is up here in Fife.'

Turner was quiet for a moment. 'A copycat?'

'We don't think so, but we're not sure. Ninety per cent sure it's the real deal.'

'Tarot card?'

'Check.'

'Broken wristwatch with time of death?'

'Also check.'

'What makes you think it might not be our guy?'

'The depth of the cut of the symbol carved into her forehead. I have the DCI up from Halifax who, like me, worked on the case when he was younger. He seems to think that it might not be the real McCoy because of the depth. I'm leaning towards it's the real thing.'

'I remember the bastard went north, and we could never figure out why. Lots of speculation, mind, but nothing concrete. I reckon he had family up there if you remember. He knew how to get about the place without getting caught. It was like he had local knowledge.'

'I remember your theory, and for what it's worth, I think you're right. I thought you were right at the time, but unless we got an arrest, there was nothing else to go on. No clues led up there.'

'Let's just say he's back after twenty years. Do you reckon he's been inside?'

'We're checking. The boss in my old unit is checking it out,' Craig said.

'It shouldn't be too hard to figure out; this guy must have been champing at the bit to get going again if he's been inside. He might plan his kills in advance and give himself time between each pair, but this would be like a horse waiting for water. He'd want it right away.'

'I agree. But he might not have been in prison.'

'Not much else left for him to have been doing. He didn't die, so that leaves moving away for a job. But don't get bogged down in the details, Jimmy. If the guy went away for twenty years and came back, he's older now. Maybe he can't put pressure down on a knife like he used to.'

'I'm taking that into consideration, but this bloke from Halifax is leaning towards a copycat.'

'Then 'e's a fool, mate. You can't be complacent. Maybe the killer wants you to think he's a copycat to throw you off the scent.'

'That had crossed my mind. I mean, how would a copycat know all the details?'

'Maybe one of the old team was talking about the case and let slip some details. Some of those female reporters would do anything for a good story. Some of the lads liked to brag, like they were big men chasing down some nutter who was carving women up. You know how it goes, especially with the younger detectives: bravado.'

'But would they go into the minute details of the killings? I'm not so sure.'

Turner was silent for a moment before speaking. 'If it really is our guy up there, then you have to think about the reason he's gone north.'

'What would that be?' Craig asked.

'You.'

FIFTEEN

'Does he know you?' DSup Calvin Stewart asked for the millionth time.

'Fuck me, I've already told you: I've seen him in the canteen a couple of times. He doesn't know me from Adam, so we're fine.'

They were sitting in a car parked in a side street off Shandwick Place in Edinburgh's West End – Stewart, DCI Harry McNeil and pathologist Finbar O'Toole.

Stewart turned to look at Harry in the back seat. 'You shouldn't be here, Harry, son. You should let me and Fin have a word with this prick.'

'I'm here to make sure you don't kill the bastard,' Harry said. 'It's just going to be a quick word.'

'If you say so.'

They bailed out of the car. The evening had got a bit cooler, and they were all dressed smart-but-casual. They walked round the corner to the club that they'd watched their target enter five minutes before.

They were walking up to the door when one of the bouncers put out a hand to stop Stewart, who was in front.

'Whoa there, Grandpa. This is a club for a younger crowd. Why don't you and your wee chums take a hike and find a nice old-timers' bar?'

'Cheeky bastard,' Harry said.

'Aye, ya big fucking ape,' Finbar said. 'Why don't you get out of our fucking way?'

The man was big, with a shaved head and a face that looked like it had stopped the front of a bus.

'Listen, ya wee shite –' the bouncer started to say, moving past Stewart, but Stewart put out his hand and stopped him. Ape tried to grab Stewart's hand, but the DSup merely grabbed hold of Ape's hand and twisted it. His friend stepped forward to help, but Finbar flicked the man hard in the bollocks, and the bouncer let out a squeal.

A third man stepped out of the club – older, wiser.

'What the fuck is going on here?' he said. 'Pair of daft bastards. This is Detective Superintendent Stewart, a personal friend of mine. You! Baw-jaws, relax or he'll have your fucking arm out of its socket.'

Stewart let the younger man's arm go and the bouncer rubbed it. Stewart grinned.

'You ever try and grab me again, and you'll be wiping your arse with your feet. You got that, son?' Stewart stepped forward and shook the older man's hand. 'Greg. Good to see you again, my friend. How's the wife?'

'Brand new, Mr Stewart, thanks for asking. How about yourself?'

'Lynn's doing well. I have to say, I thought you would have given the young boys there a heads-up.'

'I told them, Mr Stewart. Do they pay attention? Do they fuck. And you, squeaky baws, apologise to that man. Insulting him like that. And stop squealing like a wee lassie.'

'Sorry. I didn't mean what I said.'

'Apology accepted,' Finbar said.

Greg stepped forward. 'Mr McNeil, I'm sorry, I didn't recognise you there.'

'Hope you're having a good night, Greg,' Harry said.

'Listen, gents, I can get you comped at the bar.

Tell the barman, Jackie, to put your drinks on my tab. He'll know what to do.'

'That's very kind of you, Greg, son. Don't mind if I do,' Stewart said.

The three men walked in, and Stewart heard Greg say to the other two, 'Stupid bastards. You know who that is? He could bring a fucking firestorm down on both of you. He's one copper you don't want to fuck with. Nor Harry McNeil. Think yourself lucky, and if the boss finds out what you did, well, I don't need to tell you what will happen.'

The music was loud but not ear-bleedingly loud. This was aimed at an older generation who liked to have a conversation.

'You didn't tell me we were expected tonight, Calvin,' Harry said.

'I wasn't sure this was going to pan out, Harry. After you called today, I had Fin go up to the Royal. He wasn't due to do a postmortem and he was technically finished for the day, but if anybody asked, he was doing a job for me for a case we're working on.'

'What case?' Harry asked.

'I was winging it, Harry. After your pal called from Fife, I wasn't sitting about with my thumb up my arse. Besides, when I spoke to Fin and he said he'd met this lassie before, I knew we weren't going to be trudging about tonight like a bunch of twats who can't get a ride. So I had the wee man go up to the Royal.' Stewart looked at Finbar. 'Tell him what you got up to, Fin.'

Earlier that day

'Jesus, Fin, you been working out or something?' Staff Nurse Julie Compton smiled at Fin as she sat down opposite him in the café.

'I have actually,' he replied. 'My wife said I should start exercising, and eating more healthily, so I joined a gym.'

'I can tell. If you weren't married, I'd insist that you jump my bones.' She grinned at him and drank some of her coffee.

'Oh, well, you know, another time and place.'

'You can tell I'm horny. I haven't been out with anybody since that loser.'

Jesus. 'You and Monty not made up then?' He sipped his coffee.

'Wanker. I bumped into him in a bar one night, and I realised that I missed him. I thought about asking if he wanted a drink, but then this little bimbo came bouncing out of the toilets and slipped an arm through his. Big tits, teeth to die for, and a smile that would suck you in and blow you out in bubbles. I mean, what chance do I have against that? And she's fucking blonde. I mean, what chance do I have, Fin?'

'Christ, Julie, you're a very attractive woman. Don't let men take advantage. Be strong, and don't let them run all over you.'

'I wish you weren't married,' she said to him. 'You're the man I've been waiting for, but when I meet you, you're already spoken for. You know what they say about all the good ones being taken.'

Finbar was starting to think that Stewart's plan was going down the toilet, but then Julie reached a hand over and squeezed one of his and said, 'Sorry, Fin. I'm just venting. What is it you wanted to talk to me about?'

Finbar didn't move his hand. He looked her in the eyes. 'I want to talk about *him*. I need to have a talk with him but not on hospital grounds.'

She took her hand back and looked at him. 'Not about dumping me?'

'No, no. We think he's been up to capers with his ex-wife. Being a menace.'

She shook her head. 'I thought there was something not quite right with him. What do you want me to do, Fin?'

He told her.

Present

Harry had been in worse places. The only smoke was from a machine to add a little atmosphere, the music was pleasant and fast, and there was plenty of room on the dance floor.

'Do you see her, Fin?' Stewart asked, leaning in so he didn't have to shout.

'Fucking hell, make it look like you're asking me to dance, why don't you?' Finbar said.

'Shut your hole. Do you fucking see this lassie or not?'

'Aye, aye, she's over there, sitting with another lassie from work. I told her it was maybe better if she didn't come here by herself. Oh, and that you'd be paying for a taxi for them after this.'

'I bet you fucking did.'

'Small price to pay, Calvin,' Harry said.

'We could go halves on the fare, Harry,' Calvin suggested.

'And have people think you're a cheapskate? I couldn't do that to you, pal. Now, how about getting these free drinks Greg is going to pay for?'

'Aye, let's at least get a pint in our hands.'

They walked across to the bar and saw a barman with a ponytail and glasses.

'You Jackie?' Stewart asked.

The man looked at them. 'Who wants to know?'

'I'm Calvin Stewart, son. A friend of Greg's.'

The man's eyes went wide for a second. 'Oh, right. Yes, sorry. We get a lot of arseholes in here. What're you gentlemen having?'

'Three pints of lager, son.'

Jackie poured the pints and handed them over. Julie slipped up behind Fin, pinching his backside. The smaller man nearly sprayed his lager out. He swallowed instead.

'Julie! This is Calvin and Harry.'

She smiled at them. 'Nice to meet you gentlemen.'

'Likewise,' Harry said.

'Pleasure,' Stewart said. 'Thanks for helping us out.'

'Trust me, the pleasure's all mine.' She looked at Fin. 'Fancy buying a girl a drink? I'm going to need three. Two for me and one for my friend.'

Fin smiled at her. 'No problem. Tell Calvin what you want. Drinks are on him.'

'Two G&Ts and one glass of red wine.'

Calvin called Jackie over and ordered the drinks. 'We'll bring them over, Julie. Go and sit with your friend.'

'Thanks, Calvin, you're a doll.' She walked away.

'What did she say?' Stewart said. 'I didn't hear her for the music.'

'I think she called you a dildo,' Finbar said.

'Away and don't talk shite. I'll stick a fucking dildo up your arse in a minute.'

Two women were approaching them, and one was about to ask if they were dancing, but then they turned and walked away.

'Tell me again what he looks like,' Harry said to Fin.

'Attention span of a dug's curly wurly,' Stewart said.

'What does he look like, then?' Harry replied.

'There's no need to lash out, Harry. I know you've been under a lot of stress recently.'

'Don't talk pish.'

'He's over there,' Fin said. 'Monty Price. Sitting in a booth. Dark hair, blue shirt, khaki chinos. Thinks he's cool but dresses like he stepped into a time-machine wardrobe. The eighties are calling and want their clothes back.'

'The one with the little blonde next to him in the booth?' Harry said.

'Bingo.'

They walked across to a spot where they could watch him and see Julie as well. The nurse was looking across at Monty Price and looked like she could bite a chunk out of her glass and not feel it. Her eyes were laser focused and she didn't take them off her former boyfriend for one second.

Price got up out of the booth. They could see he had an empty glass in front of him. Julie saw him get up and she stood up from her table and walked across towards him, cutting him off before he could reach the bar.

The three men put their glasses down and moved away from where they were standing.

Julie approached Price and pretended to trip and threw the glass of wine over the front of his trousers.

'What the fuck?' he said, looking at her. 'Julie? What the hell?'

'Monty? Oh God, I am so sorry.'

'I bet you are. Clumsy cow.'

She grinned as he walked away, then she went to sit with her friend.

When Price walked into the men's room, Finbar was standing at the sink washing his hands. 'Jesus, what happened to you?' he asked Price.

'What does it fucking look like? Some stupid tart threw a drink over me.'

Finbar looked at the red wine stain on the front of Price's trousers.

'Why don't you take a photo?' Price said. 'It lasts longer.' He turned on a tap and started splashing water on his crotch, trying to dilute the dark-red stain that was there.

Then Finbar stepped away from the sink as he heard two bolts being unlatched. Price still had his face in a sink as the two figures approached and stood behind him.

He looked up and saw two men wearing a stocking over their heads. He gasped just as one of them, the bigger one, grabbed him by the collar and belt and bundled him into one of the cubicles.

Stewart held him while Harry kicked the back of Price's knees, and Price fell down, kneeling in front of the toilet.

Price yelled, 'Please! I have money.'

'We don't want your fucking money,' Harry said.

'What do you want, then?'

'We're here to give you a message: stop calling your ex-wife in the middle of the night,' Stewart said.

'What? I don't call her.'

Stewart forced the man's head down the toilet and Harry flushed it. Price started screaming and choking, then Stewart pulled him back up.

'You're a fucking liar. I can do this all night, pal,' Stewart said.

'Alright, alright, it was just a prank.'

'A fucking prank? You call sending her threatening letters a prank?' Harry said. 'Sick bastard.'

'I didn't send letters, I swear.'

'You hear that?' Stewart said to Harry. 'He swears.' He shoved Price's head down the pan again, and Harry obliged with the flushing.

'Here's the thing,' Stewart said, 'we don't believe you. So this is how we move forward: you don't write, or call, or do anything to piss off our friend, or else we'll come back, and not only will we fucking waterboard you, I'll kick you in the fucking bollocks so hard, your balls will swell up so much you'll be able to use them for hot-air ballooning. Do you understand me?'

Price's head was given another wash courtesy of the flushed water.

'No more presents, no more letters, no more phone calls. Do you fucking understand me?' Stewart said.

'It was just a couple of phone calls when I was drunk,' Price said when Stewart brought him back up.

'You won't speak to her ever again. Let this be a warning,' Stewart said. 'We know who you are, where you live, where you work. If we ever have to come back and have a word, it won't be to stick your fucking heid down the toilet. And I promise you one thing: you'll never see it coming.'

He and Harry stepped out of the toilet, and Finbar stepped in and kicked the man between the legs. 'That's for the photo comment.'

Price yelled and fell forward over the toilet as Harry and Stewart took the stockings off their heads.

They walked back to the dance floor, to the table where Julie and her friend were sitting.

'Mission accomplished,' Finbar said. 'Thank you both so much. But I would advise getting out of here. There's going to be a lot of shouting in here very shortly.'

The two women drank up and they all left the club.

'Thanks for the drinks, Greg,' Stewart said to the doorman as they left. The others carried on, but Stewart doubled back for a second, the younger bouncers moving out of his way.

'And don't forget, we weren't here,' Stewart said.

'Goes without saying, boss.'

SIXTEEN

Lance Harrison sat back in the booth and put his arm along the back, smiling at his female companion. 'There was the time when I attended a car crash and the woman's head was in the passenger footwell,' he said, staring into her eyes to see if they would go wide. Some women reacted that way to his stories, but this one kept on smiling and didn't flinch.

'That sounds fascinating,' the woman said. 'I've never been to a crash scene before. That must have been amazing!'

'Well, I wouldn't say that it was amazing, but it was certainly different,' Harrison said, thinking that this woman might be on this side of crazy.

'It's certainly more exciting than my job,' the

woman said. 'I just sit in an office all day, typing, filing reports, making coffee.'

'Well, that's all in the past now, because I'm retired,' Harrison said.

'Why did you come to live in London?' the woman asked. 'Where do you come from in America?'

'New York originally, but I came over here when I was a little boy with my parents. My dad was in the Air Force, so we travelled a lot.' His mobile phone rang. 'Please excuse me,' he said, taking his arm off the back of the seat and reaching into his pocket. He took out his phone.

'Hello?' he said, not recognising the number.

'Lance! It's Barry Norman. How are you doing, my friend?'

'Hey, Barry, what's up? Good to hear from you.'

'If I'm not disturbing you, I'd like to talk about one of your old cases. Well, actually, one of *our* old cases.'

'Really? Which one?' Harrison asked.

'Starman,' Norman said.

'Starman? That was a long time ago. I haven't heard that name in ages. Have you caught him?'

'I know it was. Twenty years ago. No, we haven't

caught him. He's back. In Fife, where James Craig moved to.'

Harrison looked at the woman and smiled, then stood up and walked away from the table. 'Jesus, Barry. How do you know it's him?'

'He left his signatures. Do you remember what he did?'

'Of course I do: he carved a star into their foreheads, and left an old watch on their wrists set to their time of death. Jesus Christ. And you're sure it's not a copycat?'

'None of that information was released to the public.'

'And the tarot card?'

'Yes. One of those too.'

'Good God. I wonder why he's striking again after such a long time?' Harrison said. 'Maybe he went to prison?'

'That's one theory.'

'What's the other theory?'

'We haven't got one,' Norman said. 'But listen, would you be interested in going up to Fife to meet Jimmy Craig and give your opinion? I'll make sure you're paid a fee, and all travel expenses will be covered. You'd be going as a consultant.'

'A little trip to Scotland? Count me in. I'll get the shuttle up tomorrow first thing.'

'Thanks, Lance.'

Harrison ended the call and sat back down. 'Now where were we?' he asked the woman.

'You were talking to me about death,' she said, smiling.

'So I was.'

SEVENTEEN

Craig sat in the bar of the golf club on his own nursing a pint, like a sad bastard. He looked at his watch again; Dan was late, which he never normally was. He called him.

'Dan? You still coming along to the boozer, mate?'

'Shite, Jimmy, I was going to call you. The wife's sick as a dog. Heid down the pan, going full tilt. I think she's got food poisoning or something. She's been feeling iffy for a wee while now, but she tried eating something and ending up tossing her bag.'

'Fuck me, that's a bit graphic, Dan, even for you.'

'Sorry, pal. I'm going to have to skip this one.'

'Aye, it happens, my friend. Don't worry about it.'

'See you Monday.'

'Aye, nae bother.' Craig hung up and sipped his beer. One of the golfers let on to him as he walked past to the bar, and Craig let on.

'Where's your pal tonight?' the man asked.

'He got called away on an emergency,' Craig told him, thinking it was a better response than 'his wife's puking her guts up'.

'Aye, shite happens,' the man said, walking away.

It does that. Craig thought about his wife, her mind full of the visit with their son in the asylum. Not the politically correct term, but that was what it was. Where they housed the nutters who had killed people.

He looked at his watch and knew Harry McNeil would be on his way out now with the two others, if everything was going according to plan. He hoped it was. Annie was a good friend, and he wanted to help her as much as he could.

Talk of the devil, he thought as she walked in. She smiled at him and came over to his table. She was wearing black jeans, a light-blue shirt and a white summer-weight jacket.

'Hi, Jimmy. I didn't realise you were coming in tonight.'

'The wife's not feeling too good, so I was meeting

Dan for a few, but his wife's...ill. I was just going to have one, then head off home. Lager from the fridge and Netflix. How about you?'

'I'm meeting Isla here. I'm a bit late. You haven't seen her, have you?'

Craig confirmed that he hadn't seen her. 'Can I get you a drink?'

'Thanks. G&T.'

He got up from his table as Annie sat down, and he went to the bar, got her drink and bought himself a whisky chaser. When he got back to the table, she had taken her jacket off and hung it over the back of a chair.

'Here's to good friends,' Annie said. They clinked glasses, and Craig hoped that whatever went down with her ex-husband that night, she would never find out about it.

'To us,' he said. 'At the forefront of keeping the world safe.'

'Amen to that.' She sipped her drink and put the glass on the table. 'What's up with Mark Baker these days?'

Craig looked at her, wondering if he should mention it, but then he figured she would find out soon anyway. 'He's getting a divorce. His wife left him for another man, and he's been looking after himself this past month or so.'

'Jesus. Poor guy. He looks a wreck.'

'He's going downhill. He needs to hit rock bottom, then he can bounce back, but he told me she's being a real bitch. To rub salt into the wounds, she met this younger guy online,' Craig said.

'Oh boy. If you'll pardon the pun.' She looked at him and smiled.

'Just don't tell him you heard it from me.'

'Mum's the word.' Her phone rang and she excused herself before answering. 'Oh crap. I guess I'll be hitting the town myself tonight then. Oh no, don't feel bad. I think there's something going around.' There were a few umms and ahhs before Annie said her goodbyes to Isla and she hung up.

'Isla's not coming, is she?' Craig asked.

'By God, no wonder you're a detective,' she said, grinning at him. 'But thanks for earwigging anyway.'

'I wasn't earwigging, but I'm sitting twelve inches away from you,' he said, smiling and giving her a *smartarse* look.

'Let me buy you another drink,' Annie said, standing up and taking her purse from her handbag.

'Whisky, thanks. Single malt.'

'I'll tell the barman to give you whatever you last had, if that's the malt.'

'It is. It has a name that sounds like somebody asking for a kebab when they're pished.'

'Kaboobypleesh.'

'That's the one. If you can pronounce that malt right first time, I'll buy your drinks for the rest of the night.'

She grinned at him and as she pronounced the name of the whisky perfectly.

'Shite,' he said under his breath, giving her money to buy the drinks.

Annie smiled and winked at him from the bar.

'Cheers,' he said as she put the glasses down on the table. 'You've pronounced that before, haven't you?'

She grinned. 'My dad was a big whisky drinker.' The smile slipped for a moment. 'God rest his soul.'

'We miss them when they're gone, don't we?'

'We do that, Jimmy. I miss my dad every day.'

'Me too.'

'You have any other family here?' she asked.

'I have two brothers. Half-brothers. My dad was married before he was with my mum, and he had two sons with his first wife.'

'Do you keep in touch with them?'

Craig drank some of his whisky before answering. 'The oldest one keeps in touch. The younger one hates me. He blames me for my father's death, though as we found out months ago, he was murdered. But my brother will blame me for our father's death until the day he also leaves this world.'

'Families.' She tutted and shook her head. 'I have a sister who I haven't seen since my dad's funeral. Bitch. Her and that arsehole husband of hers. Their loss, not mine.' She raised her glass. 'Here's to family who are gone but who loved us when they were here.'

He clinked his glass with hers.

There was a moment of reflective silence before Craig spoke. 'I did a background check on Raymond Taylor, the porter in your hospital who you thought might be your stalker.'

Annie put her glass down on the table and looked at him. Her hand shook slightly. 'Hit me with it.'

'He has no criminal record. Nothing. He lives with his mother in Cardenden. Never married. He might have a girlfriend, but there's no way of knowing.'

'I'd bet you a month's pay he *doesn't* have a girlfriend.'

'He's never had a parking ticket, and as far I can tell, he leads a normal life.'

Annie drew in a breath and let it out slowly before picking up her drink again. 'He seems normal to everybody in the hospital too. I asked a friend of mine and she asked some people on my behalf – you know, just to get a feeling for him. He's quiet. That's what everybody says about him. He doesn't cause trouble, is never late, he's never off sick, apparently. Jesus Christ. Maybe I got it all wrong about him.'

'Maybe he really was just sitting in your office, resting his knee.'

'Oh, Jimmy, if it's not him, and it's not my ex – although the bastard *was* calling me in the middle of the night – then who is it?'

'Did you hack somebody off at the hospital? A patient's relative, I mean.'

'Not that I know of.' She shook her head and held on to her glass, staring off into space for a moment. 'Sorry, Jimmy, I'm going home. I don't want to be out here.' She polished her drink off and reached over for her jacket.

'I'm off too. How about we share a cab?'

She stood up and put her jacket on. 'I'd like that, thanks.'

Craig had the barman call one for them. Outside,

the cool evening air had rain in it. They waited for a few minutes, and then the cab pulled up.

'I hope Isla gets better,' Craig said.

'I'm sure she'll be fine,' Annie said, getting in the back as Craig held the door open. He got in beside her and she told the driver the address, even though the barman had already done that.

Annie lived in a modern house on the north side of Dunfermline. Her Audi was parked in front of one of two garage doors.

'See you Monday,' he said to her as they pulled up outside.

'Would you mind coming in with me? Just to make sure it's safe?' She looked at him, then at the driver looking at her in the rearview mirror, then at Craig again.

'No problem.' He paid the driver and gave him a good tip, and they got out.

'This is a nice place,' Craig said as he stood in her living room. It was minimalistic, and he wondered if her ex had taken half the furniture or if this was how she had always lived.

'Thanks. This is my place. The house I shared with Shagger McGee was on the other side of Dunfermline. I wanted to get away from neighbours who would point and say, "That's the cow who got divorced from that nice laddie."'

'They didn't say that, did they?'

Annie busied herself closing the blinds and putting on a couple of lamps. 'No, they didn't say that. It was all in my head. Take a seat.'

He sat on a cream leather couch that had an end table next to it. He liked her large-screen TV, currently sitting silently over in the corner. There were a couple of prints on the wall, one of them of a seashore, the other of the countryside.

'I look at them and do "Eeny, meeny, miny, moe" when I can't decide if I want a beach holiday or a hiking holiday.'

'Really now?'

She laughed. 'No, not really. Hiking? Jesus. No, I'll take a seaside holiday any time, and not in Portobello. Drink?'

'Do you have anything that you can't pronounce the name of?'

'Nope.'

'Whisky then, thanks.'

She left the living room to go to what he presumed was the kitchen, and she came back with two glasses and a bottle.

'Do you ever have it on the rocks?' she asked, pouring two measures.

'That would be sacrilege,' he said, looking at the label and knowing that this whisky wasn't exactly cheap.

'It was my dad's favourite and I decided to keep on buying it after he passed. He was the one who got me onto it.'

'Here's to your dad. A man with great taste.'

They clinked glasses, and Craig felt the smoothness of the liquid slide down his throat. He stared off into space for a moment, before putting the glass down on the table.

'What's the matter?' Annie said. 'Are you worried what your wife might think? About you seeing me into the house?'

'Not at all. I don't have to ask anybody's permission.' He shook his head. 'I got another letter today. I get them regularly. They're from the father of the team member who was killed by a serial killer in London. She was a great detective, and I was gutted when I found out she'd been murdered, but her father writes me these threatening letters every month or so.'

He took the letter out of an inside pocket and held it out. 'You want to read it?'

She gently took it without hesitation, then slipped the letter out of the envelope. She unfolded it and began reading.

Once again, you're still fucking here, and my little girl is in the cold ground, where you should fucking be! She was talented and would have risen further up the ladder than you, you piece of shit. You couldn't solve any crimes, that's obvious from your track record.

I blame her death on you. She's not here because you let a serial killer go. Turned a blind eye, that's what you did. I'm not turning a blind eye to what you did. I'm coming for you, James Craig. You're going to suffer what my daughter suffered. I'll see to that. Everybody will know what a useless arsehole you are.

'Holy crap,' Annie said. 'No veiled threat there. He comes right out and says it.' She looked at him. 'You could do something about this, you know. Make a formal complaint. He's making threats against you.'

Craig shook his head. 'He's angry at me because he lost his daughter. He's just venting. I don't think he'll do anything about it. He's a detective himself.

Got about three years or so until retirement. He won't do anything to jeopardise that.'

'He might be unhinged enough to do something. Grief affects people in different ways.'

'It's touching that you care so much,' Craig said, smiling.

'I do actually. I mean, you've been a pain in the arse for six months now, but I like having you around to work with.'

'Once again, you have a way with words.'

She laughed. 'Let me ask you: how seriously are you taking this letter?'

'He's been sending them to my house for the past few months. One a month for three months, then they started coming every couple of weeks. Saying the same thing. This one is different, saying he's coming after me.'

'Are you worried?' Annie asked.

'No, not really. I spoke to my old boss in London about it and he said he would have a word, but I just want to ignore it.'

'Personally, I think you should let your boss have a look.'

'I'll play it by ear,' Craig said.

'Would you like another whisky?' she asked.

'Smashing, thanks.'

He got up off the couch when she left the room and walked over to a wall unit that had a Bose CD player in it and a couple of CD holders. He was looking at the spines when she came back.

'Not many people have CDs anymore,' he said, taking the glass from her. 'Cheers.'

'Cheers.' She drank a little. 'I buy CDs online and in charity shops. Monty took all the others, so I'm starting from scratch. I mean, I listen to music online too, but I like my CDs. It's a pity car manufacturers took the CD players out of cars. That was a mistake, in my opinion.'

'I agree.' He tapped a spine with one finger. 'Monaco, "What Do You Want from Me?"'

'Have you heard of it?' she asked.

'I have.'

'Peter Hook from New Order started Monaco when they were having a break. I heard the song one day and bought the CD on eBay.' She picked up the remote for the Bose and turned it on, then selected the Monaco CD and put it in and selected track number two. 'It's a little fast but still good to dance to.' She put her glass down on the unit and held out her hand.

Craig did the same and felt a buzz inside as he took her in his arms. They slow-danced around her living room like a couple of twenty-somethings – no talking, just dancing. She looked into his eyes and pulled him closer, her lips touching his, and he didn't pull away.

EIGHTEEN

'Where are we going with this one?' Blondie asked from the passenger seat, smiling her beautiful smile at him.

'You'll see. This is going to be the best part.'

The van bumped over the uneven road, past the deserted sheds that businesses had moved into years ago, some just as quickly moving out again.

The one he wanted was way at the back. He drove along the dirt track that bordered the makeshift car park, which was no more than an area of grass that was kept mowed down.

The big shed was in front of him. He skirted it and headed towards the back. The shed here had walls and doors made of corrugated iron.

'What about security?' Blondie asked him.

'What security?' he laughed in the darkness as he turned off the lights and brought the van to a stop.

He got out, taking the bolt cutters with him, and easily snapped the padlock that held the doors together. He only needed to open one, and it easily slid open, revealing the buses inside.

Blondie was standing at the back doors of the van waiting for him. 'Is it going to be easy?' she asked as he opened the doors.

'Of course it is.' He grinned at her as he stepped into the van. Under the pile of sheets lay the dead girl. There were paint cans and ladders and the sheets in case some nosy copper pulled him over and looked inside. He'd also put a piece of beef in here and let it rot. If said nosy copper smelled something, he would 'find' the meat. Say it had got lost when he did a run to the butcher and he couldn't find it. So far, no nosy copper had pulled him over.

'This is exciting,' Blondie said.

'It is. And when this is done, we can be together, just you and me. Away from everything, where we can do our own thing and nobody can take it away from us again.'

She giggled. 'I'd love that.'

He threw the sheets aside, revealing the body that lay there motionless. He dragged the dead girl towards the back of the van, jumped down and then pulled her out, lifting her in his arms.

They went inside the shed, where the buses were lined up on either side, waiting for passengers who were never going to come again.

NINETEEN

'Full Scottish breakfast?' Biggie said, carrying his tray over to the table. 'What's the difference between Scottish and English?'

They were in Morrisons at the Gyle Shopping Centre, in the cafe.

Tom Bailey was carrying a tray too. He'd chosen items from the 'build your own breakfast' menu.

'It's the same stuff,' he said as he sat down opposite Biggie. 'Except for flat sausage. All looks the same to me. Stop moaning and get tucked in.'

'I'm not moaning, boss. I was just wondering what the difference was. Like, why don't they just call it a full breakfast?'

'It's Saturday morning, and I'm usually still

tucked up in bed with the wife, but here I am, stuck having breakfast with you. Just be grateful you're getting a good fooking meal.'

'I was up at the crack of dawn having my first coffee of the day. Not like you, still in your pit.' Biggie tucked into a piece of Lorne sausage with fried egg. 'This is good,' he said, his mouth full.

'Jesus, man, where's your fooking manners?'

An old couple sitting across the aisle looked at Bailey. 'How do?' he said to them, but they ignored him.

'I'm talking English, aren't I?' he said to Biggie, who was now washing his first mouthful down with some coffee.

'You're talking loudly, and you sound like you're talking a foreign language, northern git.'

'Shut up, southern tosser.'

Biggie grinned. 'This is just like when I used to go fishing with my dad. We'd have breakfast –'

'Let me just stop you there, son. I'm not old enough to be your dad. So no comparisons.'

'We'd have breakfast in a little caff before we headed to the river,' Biggie said, carrying on as if Bailey hadn't said a word.

'Shut your hole about fooking fishing.'

'You should try it sometime. It'll take away all that pent-up frustration you're feeling.'

'Bollocks. You wouldn't get me touching a bloody fish. I don't mind eating the bastards, but I'm not touching them.'

Biggie laughed as he tucked in again. 'Big Jessie.'

Bailey looked at the younger detective. 'What do you reckon? Starman. Real or copycat?'

'I'm leaning towards real,' Biggie said, waving a piece of Lorne sausage on the end of his fork. 'Has to be. There's too many things that were part of the original case for it to be a copycat: the symbol carved into her forehead, the tarot card and the watch.'

'Aye, that's what's been getting me. You know, he operated in London, then in our neck of the woods, and now in Scotland. What if he had, or still has, family in Halifax, but then went to prison? Now he's out and he's itching to get going again. Maybe he has family up here, so up he comes and starts killing again,' Bailey said.

'Could be. Or maybe he just wants to stay away from his old hunting grounds. Makes it more difficult if there's somebody else looking for him. They don't have all the old info on him.'

Bailey nodded in agreement. 'I want to go over to

Burntisland today and see this fairground for myself. And the cemetery. Just to get a feel for things.'

'Good idea. Get some candyfloss while we're at it.'

'Fat bastard.'

TWENTY

'I just want to make sure I've got all my ducks in a row,' Arthur Jones said as his old banger juddered down the lane towards the bus museum.

Brian Hall sat back in his seat and hoped a spring wouldn't come through the seat and give him a rectal exam. 'Your son has everything in hand.'

The museum's summer season was in full swing, and it was open every Sunday through October. This was a chance to draw in visitors and make some money so the museum could keep its collection of vintage and old buses running.

Both men spent an inordinate amount of their free time working on the buses they owned. Other people owned some of the other buses, and would regularly work on them too.

'My son's a good lad, but there's so much work to be done. He can't be slacking off,' Jones said. The museum is doing well, the café's making money, and the gift shop is doing a roaring trade. But we can't sit on our laurels, Brian.'

'The bus is coming along fine, Arthur. Just wee finishing touches and we'll be able to put her out into the museum next week.'

Jones turned round the corner of the shed and jammed the brakes on. 'Fuck me,' he said.

Hall looked out the windscreen at the tall doors. One of them had been slid open. 'Do you think old McDougal was here and forgot to lock up again?'

'Clumsy old bastard,' Jones said, pulling the handbrake up like he was trying to rip it out of the car. They both opened their doors and stepped out into the warm morning sunshine.

'Aw, what the fuck?' Jones said. He stood by the front of his car, looking between the door and Hall. 'There better not be any damage. Not one fucking bit. Or else he'll be paying for it.'

'How can he pay for all the time we've spent on our buses?' Hall said. He, Jones and Jones's son owned three double-decker buses, but they'd only finished restoring one of them.

'I'll burn his bus down to the ground. I don't care

if he uses a walking stick; I'll break it over his head and shove the remainder up his arse.'

The two old men walked slowly forward, but then Hall stopped. 'Here! What if there's some bastard still inside? Taking a shite or something?'

'What do you mean, taking a shite? There's no toilets in there,' Jones replied.

'I mean taking a shite in our bus! There are dirty bastards who do that kind of stuff. One Friday night when I was a driver in Longstone, some clarty fucker had a shite in a cardboard box up the top deck. Away at the back. Fucking bus was stinking when I went up to check there were no stragglers when I got back down from Wester Hailes.'

'Och, away. Surely somebody wouldn't have a jobby in Betty?' Betty was the name of the restored bus, a 1978 Leyland Atlantean.

'Piss, jobby, puke. You name it, I've seen everything,' Hall said.

Jones envisioned a man crouched down trying to take a dump while he was tossing his bag. 'I think I would kill the bastard,' he said, his voice low and menacing. 'In self-defence, of course.'

'Of course,' Hall confirmed.

'Right, let's get inside,' Jones said, walking towards the open shed door.

'Shouldn't we call the polis first? You can see the padlock's been cut.'

Jones stopped. 'What do you think they'll do? Call out forensics and have them brush the padlock for fingerprints? Naw. Let's just hope they had a quick look around and scarpered after they found nothing worth stealing.'

He started walking forward again, Hall close behind, and they entered the huge shed. It didn't look like somebody had dropped troo and let one fly, but there was only so much natural light getting in.

Jones walked over to the light switch panel and started flicking them on. One by one, the overheads came on, the light bouncing off the gleaming Betty, who sat behind the first bus in line. They could only see the width of her as they walked down.

'Seeing these buses sitting like they're in a depot waiting to go out fills my heart with pride,' Hall said. 'I hope some bastard didn't desecrate it.' Then he stopped.

'What's wrong? Do you see somebody in there?' Jones asked, now wishing that he hadn't been hasty in saying he would deal with any bastard who'd broken in.

'I do. But I don't think she's taking a shite,' Hall said. Then he turned away and puked.

TWENTY-ONE

Craig woke to light streaming in through the bedroom window. He looked at the ceiling, then to the curtains, which had been drawn, the blinds behind them tilted horizontally just a bit so he wasn't blinded. He didn't recognise the curtains at first, and thought that Eve had maybe bought new ones. But she was staying in a flat near Carnwath in Lanarkshire, near the State Hospital.

So where was he?

'Morning,' Annie Keller said, coming in with two mugs of coffee. She put one down on the nightstand next to Craig.

'Thanks,' he said, wincing as he moved his head.

She was wearing a dressing gown and slippers. Her hair was ruffled but still looked good.

'Listen, Annie, about last night...' he started to say, but then stopped. What could he say?

She sat on the side of the bed and smiled at him. 'We made love all night. Did you enjoy it?'

Craig looked at her before turning away to drink some of the coffee. He didn't have an answer, especially since he couldn't remember any of it.

Annie laughed. 'We didn't do anything, silly bugger. Yes, we danced, and yes, I kissed you, but that was all me. I apologise. I was feeling lonely, and it's been a very long time since I had a man in my arms.'

'No need to apologise,' Craig said. 'I didn't exactly fight you off.'

'That's good, because not many men have fought me off in my lifetime. Not that I dated a platoon of the Scots Guards or anything.'

'I have to admit, it felt good to have a woman want me to hold her,' Craig said.

'Uh, hello. You have one of those at home.'

'I also have a car and I get as much attention from that as I do from my wife. I know what she's been going through with Joe, but our son can't be her sole priority.' He looked at her. 'Christ. Finn!'

'You called your dog-sitter, who promised to pick him up from your house and take him home,' Annie reassured him. 'We were wasted, I admit that. I suggested you stay over since Eve isn't home.'

'Thank you. Christ, I hope I didn't make a fool of myself.'

'In what way?'

'Like, dancing on your coffee table.'

Annie laughed. 'We polished off the whisky, but it wasn't a full bottle. It was a ratio of two-to-one, in your favour. No dancing on tables. Just the living room carpet.'

He drank some of the coffee, which was really good, then he looked at his phone, which had somehow managed to get onto the nightstand. There were no messages. He'd have to call Heather later about Finn.

'What did I tell the dog-sitter? Do you remember?'

She smiled her cheeky smile, and he knew that if life were different, he could fall in love with this woman. Not that he didn't love Eve, but ever since they'd found out about Joe being a killer, she had turned off any feelings she had for Craig.

'You told her that you'd been drinking with one of your colleagues and you were going to be late. Asked if she'd mind picking Finn up, and said you would take care of her. She was quite happy to.'

'Thank God for that.'

'You didn't lie to her. You *were* drinking with one of your colleagues. Me.'

He nodded and drank some more coffee, starting to feel more human again.

'I'm glad you came into my life, Jimmy Craig. Even as a friend. A drinking buddy. I just want you to know that.'

'Likewise. Besides, you're a better kisser than Dan Stevenson.'

She laughed and patted him lightly on the arm.

He looked at her. 'Am I...er...under the covers...I don't want to look.'

'You have your boxers on. You undressed yourself and climbed into bed yourself. Your clothes are on the radiator. I folded them after you sort of abandoned them on the floor.'

'Thanks.' His phone dinged as a text came in. He looked at it. 'Shite. It's Dan. His ears must have been burning. I have a shout.'

He threw the covers back and winced as he made to get up. 'Paracetamol?'

'In the kitchen. I'll leave the bottle out.' She heard her own phone dinging. 'I think we're going to the same place.'

She took her phone out of her dressing gown pocket and looked at it. 'Bus museum?'

Craig nodded. 'Christ, I feel ill. I don't think I can drive. Now what?'

She smiled. 'You had one too many at home. Unless one of your team speaks with your dog-sitter, nobody will know the difference. You called me to talk about Andrea Moss, mentioned you were hungover, and I offered to drive you and swung by your place to pick you up. I'm sure somebody could pick holes in that story if they really tried, but nobody will. Get dressed, Tiger. You're going to see how Auntie Annie drives.'

'Oh shite.'

'Don't mention it.'

She left the bedroom and went into her own bedroom. Craig didn't remember last night, and she wasn't going to fill in the blanks. After all, she was the one who'd got the ball rolling. As it were.

TWENTY-TWO

DS Dan Stevenson had been left instructions to call DCI Tom Bailey from Halifax if a second victim had been found. Now Bailey and Biggie were standing looking at the old bus with the rest of Craig's team.

The dead girl was sitting behind the wheel, like she was about to drive off and leave a running pedestrian behind.

'How many times have you run for a bus and the bastard's pulled away?' Bailey said to Dan.

'Too many times.'

'I think they teach them how to do that at driver training school,' Bailey said, watching the forensics crew finishing up on the bus.

They heard a car drawing up outside and saw

Annie Keller step out. Then the passenger door opened and Craig stepped out.

'Pathologist,' Dan said, looking puzzled.

'Does Jim always get a lift from her?'

'Not always.' He looked at Bailey. 'Not ever.'

Annie grabbed her things from the boot of her car while Craig walked inside.

'Morning, Dan. Tom.'

'Hey, lad, you look rougher than a badger's arsehole.'

'I had a few last night.'

'Good for you.' Bailey nodded towards the driver's cab of the bus. 'We got your second victim.'

'Christ.' Craig took a step closer and looked at the star symbol that had been carved into the girl's head. Her face was waxy pale, but he could tell it was Norma Baxter from the photo Moss had shown him.

Stan Mackay, head forensics officer, stepped off the bus. He was dressed in a white paper suit, and Craig wondered if he'd recognise the man in the street with normal clothes on.

'Hi, Jimmy.'

'Morning, Stan.'

Mackay looked at them as Annie came in, hauling her things. 'It's the same as the last one:

carved symbol, throat slashed and an old-lady watch on her wrist.'

'What's the time on it?' Annie asked.

'Eleven ten.'

'If it's from the same night, and I'll be able to tell, then it looks like they were killed within minutes of each other.'

Isla came out from behind the bus, where she'd been speaking with a tech.

Craig called her over. 'Can you contact the Moss family and tell them we think we found their daughter's friend. They'll have to identify her.'

'Sure.' She leaned in closer. 'You might want to pop a mint, sir.'

'Christ, I don't have any.'

Craig felt his arm being nudged. He turned to see Bailey holding out a packet of mints. He took one. 'Cheers, Tom.'

'I'm just jealous. I was fooking sober last night.'

'I'm not doing much for the Scottish reputation. Drunken bastard.'

'We all go there, pal.'

Isla walked away and Craig stood looking at the dead girl still sitting in the bus. 'Where was your second victim found in Halifax?' he asked Bailey.

Bailey looked him in the eyes. 'In a bus depot.

Throat slashed, watch, tarot card. It was a small satellite depot, so we figured the bastard might have family in the area and that's how he knew about the depot.'

'He's reconstructing his time in London and Halifax,' Craig said.

'I think the bastard's been away in prison. That's the only reasonable explanation,' Bailey said. He looked at Mackay. 'Did you find a tarot card on her?'

'No. We've been through her pockets, but nothing.'

'The last one was in the female's underpants,' Annie said.

They all turned round as they heard somebody shuffling into the shed. DSup Mark Baker, looking like something the cat puked up.

'Jesus, Mark, you look like something the cat puked up,' Annie said.

'You look like you've lost weight, Annie,' he said.

Annie didn't know if he was being sarcastic or not.

Craig raised his eyebrows at the boss.

'What?' Baker said. 'She knows how to use knives and shit.'

Annie pointed a finger at him. 'And don't forget

it. I'd have your willy in a stainless steel bowl before you knew what was happening.'

All the men winced.

'Fook me,' Bailey said. 'I thought our pathologist was a beast.'

'Beast?' Annie said. 'You're tall, so yours is easier to grab hold of.'

'Not now it's not,' Bailey said to Craig in a whisper. 'Fucking thing ran for the hills.' He looked at Annie. 'No offence meant.'

'Hmm. Maybe none taken. The jury's still out.' She walked forward. 'Right, Stan, let me get in there and have a wee look.' She walked past them and climbed onto the bus.

'Dan?' Craig said. 'Get the names of all the people who have access to this shed. I think the museum is only open on a Sunday, so let's get chatting to them before tomorrow. I want to know who would be here late at night and why they would be here.'

'Yes, sir.'

Annie stepped back off the bus and held up something in her hand.

'Got a spare poly bag, Stan? The Devil was in this young woman's underpants.'

Mackay stepped forward and, with a gloved hand, put the tarot card in a bag and took it away.

'It seems she died the same way as her friend, and probably at the same time,' Annie said. 'Poor girl. I'll have her on the table later and do the PM today.'

A van pulled up next to Annie's car, and Davie Cook stepped out.

'Hello, Doctor,' he said to Annie.

'Hi, Davie. She's still in place, so I'd like you to get her out of the bus and down to the mortuary. I'm sure some of the techs will help you.'

'No problem.'

Annie turned to Craig. 'Can I have a quick word, please? About the old man we had in last week.'

'Okay,' Craig said, and walked beside the pathologist towards the sunlight.

'Just walk towards the light,' she said, laughing.

Outside, the sun was shining. It wasn't as warm as Spain, but the heat felt good on Craig's face.

'Are you feeling better now?' she asked him.

'I am. Your coffee hit the spot.'

'Good. You were looking a bit white in there.'

'I think I'm feeling under the weather.'

She hesitated for a moment. 'Fancy a drink tonight?'

'Sure. How about at my place this time? That'll save me asking Heather to take Finn again.'

'Great. You can ask Isla and Dan round too, if that will make you feel more comfortable.'

'I think they're doing something else.'

'Just you and me then. Maybe Chinese?'

'Sounds good.'

She smiled at him and turned to walk away, but he stopped her. 'Just one thing. Thank you. For this morning.'

'What about this morning?'

'I think you know.'

TWENTY-THREE

DSup Barry Norman liked playing golf, but this was more important. He needed to go and see somebody.

He drove northwest from where he lived to Cricklewood. The drive took him half an hour, and he found the house easily. He hadn't been here before, but he was impressed by the semi-detached house and the nice little garden in front.

He parked behind a little Japanese hatchback. He'd had a friend once who would bring his father along for a drink sometimes, and the old boy had been in the Pacific during the Second World War and he said he would never buy a Japanese car. He hated them. He just couldn't let it go.

Norman walked up the pathway to the front door and hesitated before knocking. He could have called ahead, but why give them a heads-up? If they weren't in, he would come back later.

Just as he was about to walk away, he heard the door being unlocked. It was on a chain and a face peered round.

'Mrs Bolton? I'm DSup Norman. I worked with Sharon.'

'I know who you are,' she said.

'I was wondering if I could come in and speak to Mr Bolton. It'll only take a few minutes.'

The door closed gently, not all the way, then he heard the chain being slid along its track. The door opened all the way and Mrs Bolton stood to one side to let him in.

Norman stepped inside the house, which smelled clean and fresh.

'Through to the right,' Mrs Bolton instructed. Norman obliged and found himself in one of the cleanest living rooms he'd seen in a while.

'Have a seat,' she said.

'Thanks.' He sat in a wing-back chair that had a flowered pattern on it. There was another chair just like it, with a two-seater sofa in between. A coffee table sat in front of the sofa. A TV sat in the corner, ready to jump into action, but for now it was quiet.

'Would you like a cup of tea?'

'Thanks, Mrs Bolton, that would be smashing.'

'Edna. Call me Edna.'

She scurried away before he could use her first name. He heard her making a noise in the kitchen and hoped she wasn't raking about for the biggest knife she could find. A few minutes later, she came back with a tray with two mugs on it.

'I didn't put sugar in,' she said. 'I don't use it to be honest. Sorry.'

'It's fine, Edna. Call me Barry.'

She put the tray on the coffee table and they each grabbed a mug, and Edna sat down on the sofa.

'Jack's not here,' she said matter-of-factly.

Norman sipped his tea, hoping she hadn't put any pills in it. He hadn't seen the Boltons since their daughter's funeral and wasn't sure if they harboured any grudge against him like they obviously did against Jimmy Craig.

'Do you know when he'll be back?' Norman thought the tea was quite good. Maybe she used bottled water instead of the pish that came out of the tap.

'Can I ask what this is about, Barry?'

Norman put the mug back on the table. 'I know it was a very hard time for us all when Sharon died –'

'Was murdered.'

'– was murdered, especially for you and Jack. But as you may or may not know, DCI Craig moved to Fife –'

'We know.'

'– and he's been receiving letters. Abusive letters, from Jack. Now they've evolved into death threats. I need that to stop, Edna. It's not right, and I know it's something that Sharon wouldn't have approved of.'

'I was furious with DCI Craig. I spat in his face at the funeral, if you remember?'

'I remember that very well, yes.'

'I was angry. I had just buried my little girl. And her boyfriend, Ronnie Harper, was furious. I remember him shouting that it was Craig's fault. But you know something? Throughout all of that, Jack was the one who kept calm. He said I shouldn't have spat on Craig, and he was right. You can't un-ring a bell, and it's something I'll have to live with. Jack and I have accepted the fact that it wasn't Craig's fault. He didn't know his son was a killer, but I lashed out at him. Jack wouldn't do that. He didn't think of Jimmy Craig that way, like he was the enemy. It has to be somebody else.'

'Could Jack have maybe written those letters

without your knowledge? They started arriving at DCI Craig's new house in January.'

'He might have, but I wouldn't know. Jack walked out of my life on New Year's Eve. And I haven't heard from him since.'

TWENTY-FOUR

'You look like you lost a tenner and found a penny,' Annie Keller said, standing at the steel table.

Craig looked down at the young woman who had been removed from the bus. She'd had her whole life in front of her, but somebody had decided to extinguish it. He wanted to do things to her killer – things he couldn't and wouldn't do, but that didn't stop him thinking about what he wanted to do to the man.

'I just got off the phone with my old boss. I thought Sharon Bolton's father was the one sending me threatening letters. Turns out her father left his wife last Hogmanay and hasn't been seen since.'

'Christ. Do you still think it's him sending you the letters?'

'I have no idea. Maybe he's gone off the deep end and that's how he spends his days, writing to me.'

'What about her boyfriend? The one you told me about?'

'Ronnie Harper.' Craig blew out a breath. 'No. He had a mental breakdown and he's in a care home right now. Apparently, he can't even spell his own name, never mind write threatening letters. He hit the booze hard and was suicidal. He's a gibbering wreck, according to my old boss.'

'Jesus, that must be hard.'

'I know. I don't blame him for being angry at me. However, somebody else is pissed off at me and has been writing to me. Somebody who knows where I live.'

'That's scary.'

'I'm watching me back,' Craig said.

'I want to show you something,' Annie said to him.

He followed her back to her office, where she bent down and pulled something out of one of the drawers. She held it up for him to see.

'Chocolates?'

'They were on my desk with a little card. I pulled on some nitrile gloves before I read it. Here. Have a look.' She opened another drawer and pulled out a small envelope.

He took a pair of gloves from his own pocket and put them on, then held the envelope by its edges before sliding the card out.

'I love you. I'll do anything for you. We'll be together forever soon.' He looked at Annie. 'Were the chocolates posted?'

She gently shook her head. 'They were left on my desk.'

Craig thought about the porter, Raymond Taylor. He would seek him out and have a word with him.

They heard the lift doors opening, and she quickly took the card from him and shoved it and the chocolates into a drawer.

Two people walked into view outside her office. DSup Mark Baker looked a bit more presentable, wearing jeans and a lightweight anorak.

'Christ, Mark, you've scrubbed up a bit. Got a hot date or something?'

'I'm married,' he said, shooting a quick glance at Craig.

'Lance!' Craig said, looking at the tall American with Baker.

'Well! Jimmy Craig, as I live and breathe! How

you been, my friend?' Lance shoved past Baker and grabbed hold of Craig, hugging him. He stepped back. 'Jesus, man, you look so good.' He looked at Annie. 'Not in a gay way. Live and let live, of course, but this man is a friend of mine. We go back years. Remember the nights we had, back with the boys in Camden Town?' He laughed. 'Aren't you going to introduce me?'

'If you'll let me get a word in,' Craig said, smiling. 'Annie Keller, this is Lance Harrison. Retired pathologist. Lance, this is Annie, our esteemed pathologist.'

'The pleasure is all mine, Doctor,' Lance said, shaking Annie's hand.

'I'm Detective Superintendent Mark Baker, in case anybody's wondering.'

'We saw you there, sir,' Craig said.

While Lance and Annie chatted, Baker gestured for Craig to step out into the corridor. 'You told Annie about my wife buggering off, didn't you?'

'I did, yes.'

'Aw fuck. Now she'll think I'm some kind of loser.'

'She always thought you were a loser.'

'You're fired,' Baker said. 'No, I take that back. We need you on this case.' He nodded towards

Lance. 'He's a livewire. Bill Walker asked me to make sure he got down here to the mortuary.'

'Is he staying at your place?'

'Is he fuck. That would get the tongues wagging. Wife moves out, boyfriend moves in. No matter what I said, the damage would be done.'

'Have you tried one of those hook-up sites where you swipe when you like somebody?'

Baker grinned. 'I have. I'm meeting her tonight.'

'Jesus, you don't let the grass grow under your feet, do you?'

'Hell, no. Faint heart never won fair lady, and all that. I'm looking forward to having a bit of fun. I'm glad the old boot is gone, to be honest.'

'Sorry to interrupt your little powwow, gentlemen, but Lance would like to look at our latest victims, since he worked on the original victims,' Annie said, stepping into the corridor.

'Oh, sorry, I didn't recognise you without your white suit on,' Baker said.

'The one that makes me look like I've lost ten pounds?'

'Aye, that one.'

She looked at him before leading them through to the autopsy suite. Norma Baxter was on the table, covered in a sheet. She gently pulled it back.

'My assistant will be in shortly, but we can have a look.'

Lance looked down at the symbol carved into the young woman's forehead as Annie stepped away.

'Can you tell if this carving is deeper than the others?' Craig said. 'We're trying to figure out if this is a copycat or the real guy.'

Lance pulled out a pair of reading glasses and peered closer. He stood up and looked at Craig. 'The skin on the forehead is only about one and a half millimetres thick, so each carving is going to be the same depth, more or less.'

'Does it look like it's the same size as the others?' Baker asked.

Lance looked at Annie. 'Was this measured?'

'Yes. It's the same as the last one; exactly one inch from each point to point. He was very meticulous.'

Lance nodded. 'The exact same measurements. I'd say the real Starman is now working on your beat, Jimmy. You should contact Halifax and see what their reports say, but I'm willing to bet it's the same killer.'

'We have a couple of detectives up from there, comparing our victims to theirs from twenty years ago.'

'What about the tarot card?'

Annie stepped forward. 'I took it out of her underpants. It's with the forensics team right now.'

'The Devil card?'

Annie nodded. 'Yes.'

'It all points to the same killer, I'm afraid. The exact measurements, the tarot card, and your old boss told me that there was a wristwatch on the first victim,' Lance said to Craig.

'And on this one too.'

Lance blew out his cheeks. 'If I was a betting man, I would put my money on this being the real deal, not a copycat.'

'Why is he here?' Baker said. 'Why not London or Halifax?'

Craig looked at them. 'As my old boss said, there's one connection between London and here. Me.'

TWENTY-FIVE

Craig picked up Finn from the dog-sitter. They were standing in Heather's hallway, Finn standing next to his dad, and Craig rubbed the dog's head just under his ear.

Heather was a writer who sat in with Finn every day and used Craig's study to write in.

'How's the new book coming along?' he asked her.

'I've written a few chapters since we spoke yesterday,' she said with a laugh. Heather's husband came out of the kitchen and waved to Craig on his way to the living room, holding a plate with a sandwich on it. 'How was last night?'

Oh, let me see – my friend didn't turn up, so I got drunk with the pathologist and stayed the night at hers. I had so much fun, we're doing it at my house tonight.

'It was good. I had a little too much to drink. Thanks for stepping in. I sent you some extra money on my phone.'

'Thank you. Finn's such a sweetheart.' She looked at Craig as if she knew he was lying about what he had been doing. 'Same time Monday?'

'Yes, thank you. I don't know when Eve will be back.'

'No explanation needed.'

He took the dog and they got into his Volvo, and he drove down the road back home to Dalgety Bay. 'You won't leave your dad, will you, pal?' he said to Finn, and the dog wagged his tail from the back seat. Craig missed his wife at times, but recently, the fighting had made him glad she was staying down near Carstairs.

He let the dog have a pee on the green area across the road from the house. It was sunny and warm. He looked over to the house, and for a moment he expected to see Eve standing at the window, and he felt a kick inside.

'Come on, boy, let's get your dinner sorted.' They crossed over the road, and inside the house, the dog ran upstairs to the living room as if expecting to see his mum there, but once again he was disappointed.

Craig fed the dog and called a number. 'Harry? It's Jimmy Craig. How did things go last night?'

'Hey, Jim. Things went according to plan. A couple of friends of mine and I had a word. I don't think your pathologist will be getting any more phone calls anytime soon. He said that's all he did.'

'I appreciate that. However, she was left a box of chocolates on her desk. She assumes it was her stalker. The late-night phone calls are taken care of, but I don't think her ex is the stalker.'

'Fuck's sake. Anything I can do to help, just give me a shout, pal.'

'I will, Harry. Thanks again. I owe you one.'

Finn had finished his dinner and was playing with his ball, which he dropped for Craig to toss back to him. They played this game for a few minutes, then Craig went to wash the doggy drool off his hands.

Half an hour later, Annie appeared at his door. 'I'm doing house calls now. I heard there's a man with a super-fast pulse. I need to check him out.'

'Come in, Doctor.'

She smiled and he saw she was holding a bottle of white wine. He also noticed the taxi leaving. She saw him noticing. 'I may get boozed up tonight. I'm feeling a bit shaky.'

'I have that effect on women.'

'It was the box of chocolates that I found in my office.'

'Oh yeah, that.'

'I'm convinced it's Raymond Taylor. Davie Cook, my assistant, said he sees Taylor down in the mortuary all the time.'

They walked upstairs to the living room, where Finn rushed over to greet her. She was wearing a summer dress this time, with a light jacket.

'If you were wearing your black jeans, he'd have hair all over you. I'm not saying he sheds a lot, but sometimes it's like waking up to find tumbleweeds have blown through the house.'

'Oh, he's such a sweetheart.' She passed the wine to Craig so she could pet the dog.

Craig took the wine into the kitchen, feeling a pang of guilt for a moment. Here he was entertaining a woman in the house, while his wife was down south.

She said she wants to separate. She's not coming back. Besides, this is a colleague. The little voice in his head didn't convince him that he was in the right.

'We ordering Chinese?' Annie said, coming into the kitchen.

'Yes, we are. What's your favourite?'

'I'm having lemon chicken. With fried rice. You?'

'Sweet and sour chicken. Rice.'

'Do you want me to call it in? I know a good place in Dunfermline. They'll deliver.'

'Okay.'

He left her in the kitchen to call it in while he went into the living room. He'd been pissed off when Eve had told him a couple of months ago that she wanted to be near Joe. But Joe getting arrested and then taken out of the hospital by somebody who thought she was doing him a favour had rocked her world. Even though she hadn't given birth to their son, he was her little boy, and she was going to do what she was going to do.

His mobile phone rang.

'Hello?'

'Jimmy. It's Barry Norman.'

'Hello, Barry. How you doing?'

'Listen, son, I did something today that you might not approve of.'

All sorts of thoughts ran through Craig's mind as he stood looking out of his window at the Forth Rail Bridge. 'I'm open-minded, Barry. What you do in your own time is your business.' He was trying to keep the mood light, even though Norman didn't sound like he had been down to Brighton's seafront.

'This is serious, Jimmy. It's about the letters you've been getting.'

'What about them?'

'Let me ask you something first. When you got the letters, did you see the postmark?'

'Yes, I did. London.'

'Jesus.'

'Why, Barry?'

'Jack Bolton walked out on his wife on Hogmanay. She hasn't heard from him since. I think he's sending you the letters, but we don't know where he is. Did the *last* postmark have London stamped on it?'

'Yes, it did.' Craig paused for a moment. 'Does he have any family in the area?' Craig asked.

'You tell me, Jimmy. Jack Bolton's Scottish. He comes from Fife.'

Craig was silent for a moment. 'I never knew that. Sharon never mentioned her father was from here.'

'Sharon was a private person, Jimmy. She never wore her heart on her sleeve. She was good at her job and didn't discuss things like where her father came from.'

'If he left London on Hogmanay, could he be up here?'

'I never said he left London then. I said he left his wife then. He might still be down here. Or he might have gone north. Who knows? But he certainly knows the area.'

'Right. By the way, Lance Harrison is here. He had a look at our victim and says that the star carved on the girl's forehead measures the exact same as the ones he saw when he was the pathologist in London. It's looking more and more like it's the original killer come back. But let me run this past you.' Craig told Norman what he was thinking.

'I'll be going into the station tomorrow, then I'll call you,' Norman said.

'Cheers, Barry.'

He hung up, and Annie came through from the kitchen. 'Everything okay?' she asked.

'Not really. I just found out that Sharon Bolton's father, Jack, comes from Fife. And he disappeared six months ago.'

'He's been writing you letters and threatened you. And he knows Fife. Christ, Jim, please be careful.'

'I will be.'

'Is there anybody else in the picture?' Annie asked. 'In case it isn't him.'

'Not that I know of.'

'Just be careful, Jimmy.'

'I will.' He realised that this woman, his colleague, actually cared more about his safety than his own wife did. Should he be calling Eve his wife? he wondered. Estranged wife. That sounded more realistic.

'I ordered the Chinese. I know you asked Lance Harrison to join us for dinner, but I'm glad he didn't want to,' Annie said.

'It would have been nice to catch up with him, but I'm sort of glad too. He's going to FaceTime a girlfriend of his. He's never been a one-woman man. God knows how he does it. I'll see him again before he goes.' He looked at her. 'I'll send you the money for the Chinese.'

'You don't have to. If you buy me dinner, then you might expect something afterwards.' She grinned at him.

He smiled, but his thoughts were on somebody back in London who wanted him dead.

TWENTY-SIX

They had finished their Chinese and were walking along the Fife Coastal Path, part of which was outside his house. Finn was running about, sniffing. The evening was beautiful, the sun heading west but still glittering off the sea. Across the way, they could see Arthur's Seat in the distance, the castle a tiny blob to the right, and the islands out in the Forth.

'Makes you glad to be alive, doesn't it?' Annie said.

'It does. You should enjoy every moment, because you don't know when it's going to end.'

'Like those poor girls. Out for a night of fun in Burntisland and then boom. It was over,' Annie said. She moved a little bit closer to Craig. 'Look, about last night...'

'No words are needed,' he said.

'I think they are. I was drunk, lonely and scared.'

He smiled at her. 'And here I thought it was just my charm.'

She elbowed him. 'You know what I mean. I don't sleep around.'

'Neither do I. Eve's the only woman I've been with since before I was twenty.'

'Monty was the only man for me. Even after we divorced, I didn't want another man.'

'I'm not saying last night was a mistake,' Craig said. 'I just wish I'd been sober.'

'Jesus. You've seen me naked and you can't even remember. That's some impression I must make.'

He laughed. 'Come on, let's head back. I want to bounce some ideas off you.'

'Ooh, talking shop. I like it.'

Craig called the dog over, and he ran up to them and walked by Craig's side.

'Let me hear what you've got,' Annie said as they made their way back.

'Right. Lance said that he thinks that the original killer is up here. He thinks it has to be him, because the key elements are there: the watch, the tarot card, the manner of death.'

She was walking close to him now, like she was

expecting somebody to jump out of the bushes. 'I think you're right. If I was to hazard a guess, I'd say it has to do with Sharon Bolton.'

They made it back to the house and Finn ran upstairs.

'Can you pour us a glass of wine?' Craig asked. 'I want to make a phone call.'

Annie nodded and he went into the living room. Called Barry Norman.

'Barry? Can you give me the name of the home Ronnie Harper's in? And the number if you have it?'

'Jesus, Jimmy. You're not going to wind the boy up, are you?'

'No. But I need you as my eyes and ears down there. There's somebody killing people up here and I think you were right: this has got something to do with me.'

'Hold on.'

Norman went away for a moment and Annie came through with two glasses of white. She handed one to Craig and sat on the couch.

Craig walked over to the nook and sat down, getting a pad and pen from the little bookcase there.

'You got something to write this down with?' Norman said, coming back on the line.

'Yes. Go ahead.'

'It's the Northern Home for Rehabilitation. They take in mental health patients, amongst others.'

'Thanks, Barry. Talk to you tomorrow.'

Craig ended the call and dialled the number for the care home.

'Hello, my name is Detective Chief Inspector James Craig, from Police Scotland.'

'How can I help you?' said the woman on the other end. She sounded frazzled.

'I'm calling about one of your patients, a detective I used to work with. DS Ronnie Harper. I was wondering how he was doing. I can't visit him, so I thought –'

'I can't give you any details of any patients here.'

'Not even to let me know how he's doing?'

'Goodbye.'

She hung up before he had a chance to thank her. He sat down on the couch beside Annie and lifted his glass of wine. They clinked glasses.

'How's your friend?' she asked.

'He's not my friend. He's the one person in the world who would kill me, given half the chance.'

'He's locked up, though, isn't he?'

'According to Barry Norman. Not exactly locked up, but under supervision, yes.' He looked at her. 'I've been thinking about Starman.'

'Tell me.'

'I know Lance thinks the original guy is here, but let's play Devil's Advocate for a minute and say it's a very clever copycat. It has to be somebody who has intimate knowledge of the original crimes.' He paused for a moment. 'That would mean our killer now has inside information. He's a copper.'

TWENTY-SEVEN

The prisoner was still there, in the stall, sitting on the mattress, his head leaning over to one side now. The drugs in the water kept him from getting too adventurous and having a go.

'I've brought you a visitor,' he said, holding the dead woman in front of him like a life-sized ragdoll. He shuffled forward, feet spread out either side of her. She wasn't heavy, but the movement was awkward. Still the prisoner on the mattress didn't stir.

The man could see the bucket was full. The food hadn't been eaten, just nibbled at.

He threw the woman down on top of the man, then grabbed her hand and drew her fingernails across his cheek, drawing blood.

The prisoner flinched as if he'd been stung on the face by a bee. Hazy eyes looked at the man as he grabbed the woman under the arms and hauled her towards the door.

He turned to the prisoner. 'Don't worry. Not long now.'

Eve Craig sat back in her chair and poured herself another glass of wine. She was going through the photos on her phone, looking at herself with her husband. Back in a happier time, when they lived in London, their son was at university (although not for as long as they had thought) and Jimmy was happy in his job, as was she. There were photos of Finn growing up through the years. She found the very first one she had taken of him in the breeder's house, and thought about the beautiful boy he had grown into.

She missed her dog. More than she missed Jimmy, if she was honest. Finn would greet her in the morning by coming up to her, wanting his head rubbed. He was the one loyal male she had in her life, and it made her heart ache not to see him every day.

It was late now, but she didn't care. This was her life now: see Joe, come home, eat dinner, drink wine, rinse and repeat. She would go and see him tomorrow again, and the day after. Jimmy could come down here if he wanted, but no, having a son for a serial killer went against the grain. He wouldn't just quit the force and start a new life with her here. He could get a new job if he wanted to, something that wouldn't keep him away from her and Joe. They could be happy again, if only –

Her phone rang. She jumped, startled by the noise. She looked at the screen. It wasn't Jimmy; nor a number she recognised. She was about to ignore it, thinking it was probably spam. But what if it wasn't? What if it was the hospital?

'Hello?' she said, answering it.

'My name is Dr O'Brian. Is this Mrs Craig?'

Her heart jumped and she sat forward in her chair. The wine had kicked in hours ago, but she could make out what the man was saying. 'Yes.'

'I'm afraid there's been an incident at the hospital regarding Joe. I was wondering if you could come over straight away?'

'I've been drinking. I'll get a taxi.'

'No need, Mrs Craig. I'm on my way to pick you

up. I think it would be better if you didn't drive anyway.'

'Has something happened to Joe?'

'He's having an episode. He's holding another patient hostage. Not in a way that means we need to call the police just now. We thought if he saw you, he might calm down and we could deal with this in-house, as it were.'

'I'll be ready in five minutes.' She was about to add that she needed a pee but kept that to herself.

'I'll be there in a couple.'

He hung up, and Eve got up out of her chair and the room swam. There was no way she could drive. O'Brian was a godsend. She staggered through to the bathroom, where she peed and flushed, and then puked. She didn't go down on her knees but bent over instead.

After the second flush, she rinsed her mouth out and spat in the sink, grabbing the bottle of mouthwash that sat there. She swirled and spat again into the flow of water from the cold tap. She turned it off and looked in the mirror. Christ, she looked like a fucking werewolf.

She combed her hair with her fingers. She would tell O'Brian that she hadn't been sleeping well, that she'd been up for twenty-four hours, that was why her eyes were red. If he asked, which he probably wouldn't. Maybe he would just think that she was a lush and she'd been sitting boozing all night. Which she had been.

There was a knock on the door, and she grabbed a light jacket as she rushed over to the door, as best she could rush in the state she was in; it was more of a careful shuffling, hand out to try to stop her head from bouncing off the carpet if she should fall.

She opened the door and a man was standing there smiling at her. 'Mrs Craig?' he asked.

'Yes. Dr O'Brian?'

'One and the same.' He looked at her. 'Do you think I could come in and use your facilities?'

Eve stood looking blankly at him.

'The toilet?' he prompted.

'Oh yes, come in.'

She hadn't even managed to shut the door all the way when she felt something hard hit her in the back of the head. Then she felt nothing at all.

TWENTY-EIGHT

DI Fred Kohler was up early and driving down to South London, where the police records were stored. They were in a secure warehouse, and there was twenty-four-hour access. He'd called ahead, just to make sure nobody was sleeping on the job. He was sure that they wouldn't be, but you could never tell.

He had been told about the murder up north, that if it was a copycat, then it could be a copper. How else would they get access to the information that nobody else had? They had come in and read the case notes.

He showed his ID at the reception area and signed in. The uniformed sergeant didn't know him from Adam and looked like he needed to go home to bed.

'Long night?' said Kohler.

'Quiet night, sir.'

Kohler was shown through to the correct area of the warehouse by a younger uniform, who told him to let them know when he was leaving so he could sign out. Kohler was about to tell him that this wasn't his first visit and make a crack about his granny sucking eggs, but he let it go.

He took a box off the shelf, just one of many. It was marked 'Starman', which annoyed him. Maybe he was just getting too grumpy in his old age.

He sat at a table and took the lid off the box and started pulling out files.

He looked at the four postmortem reports. All killed the same way. All had an old watch put on their wrist, set to the time of death, according to Lance Harrison, the pathologist. And each had a tarot card in their trouser pocket.

It was a long time ago, but Kohler was taken back to that time like it was yesterday. Harrison was the best pathologist he'd ever worked with, and a hell of a nice man. Harrison would come out to the pub with them and they'd get blootered. He was one of the boys.

There was one detective who didn't like Harrison at all: DS Steve Carver. Now DCI Carver, retired. The same copper who had led Ronnie Harper away from the cemetery on the day of Sharon's funeral.

Carver had eventually transferred to another MIT, and he didn't have to see Harrison again.

Kohler was a DS at the time and had asked Carver what his beef with Harrison was.

'I just don't like him,' Carver had said. 'He's a misogynist and thinks he walks on water.'

Kohler got up from the table and put the box away and made his way to the reception area.

'Can I see the log-in book?'

'Yes, sir,' the sergeant said, handing over the thick ledger-type book. Everybody had to sign in and sign out again.

Carver had retired two months ago, around the time young Ronnie Harper had been admitted to the care home. Kohler had seen Harper before he went away. His performance at the cemetery, shouting at Craig, blaming him for his girlfriend's death, had been appalling and the young man had been on the carpet for it. Kohler had seen him at the station; the young man had red rings round his eyes from a combination of crying, lack of sleep and – something Kohler found out later – getting boozed up all the time.

Kohler skipped back through the sign-in book, going back months. He expected to see Carver's name.

He saw Jack Bolton's name.

He had signed in, requesting to see the Starman case notes.

Kohler closed the book, thanked the sergeant and left the building.

TWENTY-NINE

Craig got a call, but it wasn't from Barry Norman. Not yet. It was from Dan Stevenson.

'Dan. What's up?'

'Sorry to disturb you on a Sunday, boss, but we got a shout.'

'Give me the details, Dan.'

Dan told him where he needed to be. Craig thanked him and hung up. He walked through from the kitchen to the living room, where Annie was sitting drinking her coffee.

'Do you remember what happened last night?' she asked him.

'Of course I do. We had dinner, watched a film, had a few glasses of wine and then…then it's a blank.'

'Oh, shut up. It better not be, or else you'll be giving me a complex.'

He laughed, bent down to where she was sitting on the couch and gave her a kiss. 'I hope you're not taking advantage of me because I'm witty and charming, not to mention dashingly handsome,' he said, standing upright again.

'Now, let me think about that...Nope. It's because you're a bitcoin billionaire.'

'I knew it!' He kneeled down to pet Finn, who was lying near one of the windows. Then he looked back at Annie. 'What's bitcoin?'

Her phone rang. She answered it and spoke to the caller, then hung up and finished her coffee. 'I'm assuming we're going to the same place?' she said.

'Kirkcaldy,' Craig answered.

'Yep.' She put her coffee mug on the table and stood up. Finn got up, not sure what was going on, but if it involved a ball and going to the park, he was in.

Craig had to disappoint him. If he was going to be late, he'd call Heather.

Annie suggested that they have a race there, but he reminded her that she had come in a taxi the day before and had no car.

'That could be a problem,' she said.

He drove her home to pick up her car and then left, heading for Kirkcaldy along the A92. It was busy, even for a Sunday, and he was pretty sure he saw a dark-blue Audi saloon whizz by in a blur, but couldn't be sure. He himself was driving fast, with his blue flashers on.

He took the exit for Kirkcaldy, headed down towards the promenade and made his way to Pathhead Sands beach. A patrol car was at the entrance to the driveway that led down to the beach, and the officer waved Craig through. He drove down the road, and the sun was glittering off the water. He parked next to the other emergency vehicles and a dark-blue Audi.

He got out and walked towards a uniform standing on the pathway that led down to the sand. They nodded to each other, then Craig saw the forensics tent with the forensics guys milling about on the beach. One of the mortuary assistants was there. Davie Cook.

'How you doing, Davie?' Craig said to the younger man as he approached him.

'Not bad, sir. I could do without this on a Sunday morning, right enough, but it comes with the territory.'

Craig moved closer to him. 'What's your opinion of the porter Raymond Taylor?'

'Quiet. Bit of a weirdo. I caught him talking to a dead woman one time. Just having a conversation with her. He's one of those people you wouldn't turn your back on. Know what I mean?'

'You think he's dangerous?'

'I think there's two sides to him.'

'Thanks.'

'No problem, sir.'

Across the sea, it was basically the same view Craig had seen when he was walking last night with Annie: Arthur's Seat in Edinburgh, and East Lothian further along the coast, the Bass Rock sticking up out of the sea like the start of a mushroom cloud, frozen in time.

Dan Stevenson was waiting for Craig near the tent. 'Morning, sir. The others are talking with a group of people along the way. Most of them have dogs. One of them said his dog ran up to the girl, who was sitting with her back against a rock.'

'Is it like the other two victims?'

Dan shook his head. 'No. Completely different. There's a page from a road atlas sticking out of her pants.'

Craig was about to go into the forensics tent, but he stopped dead.

'Atlas?'

Dan nodded.

'Did you have a look at what part of the country the page shows?'

'Yes. London.'

'Fuck me.' Craig stepped inside and saw Annie and Stan Mackay. 'You got a helicopter or something?' he said to the pathologist.

She grinned at him. 'Traffic was light. Besides, I don't drive like an old granny going to church. I'm sure there were some of them on the roads today.'

She was suited up already and gave him a sly wink when nobody was looking.

'Dan told me about the map in the woman's underwear,' Craig said, looking down at the victim, who was sitting against a large rock that was a permanent feature of the beach. There it was for all to see: the coloured map sticking up out of her underwear.

Mackay nodded. 'We've photographed it, but we wanted you to see it before I bag it.'

'You look like you've seen a ghost,' Annie said to Craig.

'We had a killer in London who we were hunting. He would stab them in the heart and tear out a piece of a map from an atlas, leaving it in the victim's pocket to be found. The press called him The Atlas Killer. He killed five women over a five-year period. One a year. On the ninth of June.' He looked at his watch. 'Today is the ninth of June.'

'Fucking hell,' Dan said, his voice a whisper.

'Where does that leave us with the Starman killer?' Annie said. 'We thought it was the original killer up here, but this changes things, doesn't it?'

'It does,' Craig said. 'Was there any ID on her?'

Mackay nodded. 'Caitlin Morgan. There's a driving license with her name on it.'

'Can you give the details to Dan. He'll organise the death notice.'

'Will do,' Mackay said.

'I have to make a couple of calls,' Craig said.

Craig left the tent and walked back over the beach to his car, the gentle breeze coming in from the sea following him. He saw Max Hold walking about in the car park, talking to people. He shouted him over.

'Sir?'

'You worked with Neil McGovern, you told me. The man who runs the witness protection department in the Scottish government.'

'Yes, sir. He's a good guy.'

'I'm assuming he could cut through a lot of red tape, if you asked him?'

'I'm sure he could.'

Craig looked at Hold for a moment. 'I know it's Sunday and he's probably doing something fun right now, but do you think you could call him and ask him for a favour?'

'He has people working twenty-four seven. Whatever you need, I'm sure it's only a phone call away.'

Craig told Hold what he needed.

'I'll get right on it, sir.'

'Good lad.' Craig watched Hold walk away.

He took his phone out and saw he had missed a phone call from Barry Norman. Christ, he had silenced the phone earlier and had forgotten to put the sound back on. He dialled the number.

'Barry? It's Jimmy Craig.'

'I know it's you; your number came up on my screen. You need to keep up with the times, son. Get on board with technology. When you see a name come up, that's the person who's calling you.'

'I promise I'll look at a YouTube video tonight. I'm sorry I missed your call; my phone sound was switched off.'

'Aye. Guess what?'

Fuck. Craig hated the *Guess what?* game. Several answers sprang to mind, but none of them fitted in with the subject, he was sure. 'Tell me.'

'DI Jack Bolton was looking at the case files for Starman a couple of months before he retired.'

'Shite. I didn't work with him, but I heard the stories about him. And remember the fucking glare he gave me at Sharon's funeral down there? Ronnie Harper was standing there shouting at me, and that bastard gave me a look of pure hatred after his wife spat on me. Fucker. But let me ask you: did he know where I came from?'

'Well, Sharon was on your team, so she knew. I assume she probably mentioned it to her father, since he came from Fife too.'

'That makes sense, and then he found out I'd transferred up here. Jesus.'

'Keep me in the loop, Jimmy. Is that another Starman victim you have?' Norman asked.

'No. This is a different one entirely. You remember The Atlas Killer?'

'I do. Again, not a case I worked, but I remember.'

'He's struck again.'

'That can't be right. Another victim from a cold case?'

'I think this confirms that this is a copycat killer up here. And he's copying more than one cold-case killer.'

'You could have a point there, son. Keep in touch.'

Craig hung up and dialled another number.

THIRTY

Tom Bailey wasn't in a hurry to get home. He intended to spend as many nights here as possible. It was almost like a mini break without the wife. He and Biggie had gone for a few pints in the city centre the night before, riding the tram there and back. It stopped outside their hotel, on the other side of the tracks.

They'd had breakfast in Morrisons again, Bailey having the 'fat-bastard special', as Biggie called it.

'I'm a growing lad,' Bailey had told him.

'You certainly are.'

'Cheeky bastard.'

Now they were sitting in Tim Hortons in Fife Leisure Park. Bailey had scoffed at the idea of going for a coffee in Dobbies garden centre. The plants would rip him apart with his allergies.

'Wee lass,' Biggie had admonished, but then he'd spotted the coffee place across the road.

Now they were playing a game.

'"Zoom",' Bailey said.

Biggie shook his head. 'Come on now. The eighties is your thing.'

'I never said it was from the eighties.' Bailey sipped his coffee, which was the best he'd ever tasted.

'Is it from the eighties?'

'Yes.'

'Fuck's sake. That's borderline cheating.'

'Is it fook. Now get guessing. You already owe me twenty quid.'

'I owe you fuck all, cheating bastard.'

'How is it fooking cheating?' Bailey said, shaking his head. 'I know who Glenn Miller was, but I wasn't born when he went missing.'

Biggie tapped his fingers on the table, then rubbed his chin.

'You've got until I finish my doughnut, then it's thirty quid,' Bailey said.

'That gives me a second, then.'

'Shut your fooking pie hole and get your thinking cap on.'

'Christ, I've heard this song too.' Biggie was humming the tune. 'Ah, bollocks. I can't think of it.'

'Fat Larry's Band.'

'Figures you would know that one.'

'Shut your hole and get up there and get me another doughnut. If I was with the wife, I wouldn't dare. But since it's you, don't let the grass grow under your feet.'

Biggie made a face and got up from the table as Bailey took his phone out and sent another text to his wife. She was a little stick of dynamite, but he loved her. He hoped Biggie would find somebody like his wife.

The young detective came back with two doughnuts. 'I got myself one for going.'

'Cheers. But you can see I'm big. You're just going to be a fat bastard, since you're so short.'

'Yeah, yeah.'

Bailey's phone rang.

'Hello?'

'Tom, it's Jimmy Craig. Are you still in your hotel?'

'No, pal, me and the boy are touring Fife, taking in some of the sights. We're in Tim Hortons in Fife Leisure Park just now, having a coffee. What's up?'

'I'm at a murder scene. You got spare time?'

'I've always got time for a murder, lad. Tell me where and we'll find it.'

THIRTY-ONE

The dog walkers and others were mostly gone now, shepherded to their cars after their names were taken.

Tom Bailey walked over the sand towards Craig, Biggie in tow. Craig shook hands with the big man.

'We were just dodging about,' Bailey explained. 'Fife's got a lot of history.'

'It has that.'

'All them fooking mines closed. Shower o' shite. Still, the planet's better off, or it would be if those fook-wit politicians would stop flying around in their private jets, eh?'

'Never happen,' Biggie said, coming up behind Bailey and nodding at Craig. 'It's "do as I say, not as I do". That's why I think that not one politician is serious about climate change. They're concerned about future votes.'

Bailey looked at Biggie. 'That's enough, lad.' He turned back to Craig. 'We have debates and discussions. The boy's not a fan of politicians. Neither am I, but we have to watch what we say around the bigwigs. They're all politicians in uniform, so we keep our opinions to ourselves.'

'Same here,' Craig said. 'But listen, I called you because I want you to have a look at our victim. See if there's any similarity to a case you might have had in Halifax.'

He took Bailey and Biggie inside the forensics tent. Annie was still there, as was Stan Mackay.

'How do?' Bailey said, nodding to them. Then he stepped forward and looked down at the victim, and the piece of road atlas sticking up out of her underwear. 'Fook me,' he said, his voice barely a whisper. 'We *did* have a murder like this.'

'When?' Craig asked.

'Let me think.' Bailey looked up to the ceiling of the tent, as if for inspiration. 'Early two-thousands.'

'Jesus,' Craig said. 'Us too, in London. He killed one woman a year for five years. The press called him The Atlas Killer. Original. One wit even wrote the headline "Detectives on the road to nowhere" after we failed to catch him. Now we know he was operating in Halifax. Just like Starman.'

'It's the same killer, isn't it?' Bailey said.

'I think it is. He stopped killing them as Starman and started killing again using a different MO. The only difference now is, he's putting his signature in the victims' underwear,' Craig said. 'Why the change of MO?'

'Not sure, Jimmy,' Bailey said. 'Our lass was found by the side of a river. Facing the water, just like this one.'

'Knock-knock,' a voice said from outside. The tent flaps parted and Lance Harrison walked in.

'Thanks for coming on short notice,' Craig said, shaking the man's hand. 'I wanted you to give us your opinion, if you don't mind.'

Bailey nodded at the American ex-pathologist and stepped aside, revealing the murder victim.

'The Atlas Killer?' Lance asked Craig.

'We think so. I didn't know it until now, but Tom said he killed a woman in Halifax around the same time.'

'Is there ID on her?' Bailey asked Mackay.

He nodded. 'There was a wallet on her. She lives locally.'

'She's a nurse, isn't she?' Craig said.

'Yes,' Mackay answered. 'How did you know?'

'The first victim in London was a nurse. Then he took a teacher.' Craig looked at Bailey. 'What profession was yours?'

'A librarian.'

'They were all professional women in London. One a year over five years, then he stopped.'

'Why now?' Lance asked. 'Why up here?'

'I think I know who the killer is: DI Jack Bolton. His daughter was on my team until she was murdered. He blames me for her death.'

'Where is the bastard?' Bailey asked. He towered above everybody else and it almost seemed like he was filling the tent on his own.

'He disappeared six months ago,' Craig said. 'But he originally came from here, like I did. I didn't know that before because I didn't work with him. He was a DI in another station.'

'So he knows his way around here?' Lance said.

'I presume so.'

'Any idea where he could be?' Biggie asked.

'Not got a fucking clue,' Craig said.

THIRTY-TWO

'Wakey-fucking-wakey!'

The voice was shouting near her ear. It startled her into wakefulness, but she felt groggy and sick.

Then water was splashed over her face. She spluttered and panicked for a moment, shaking her head.

'Come on, Eve. Time to get yourself together.'

The face looking at her was smiling, but it was a mask the man was wearing. Some grotesque Halloween mask, with just eye holes. The voice was muffled a bit, but she could hear him clearly enough.

'Who are you?' she asked, as if she'd just woken up from a deep sleep.

'You don't know me, but my name's Jack.'

'Where are we?' Eve asked. Wherever it was, it stank. Like an animal had shat in here.

'Never you mind where we are. It's where you're going that counts. But first, I brought you some breakfast. Here.' He held out a McDonald's paper bag.

She felt like slapping it out of his hand, but her stomach was grumbling now, so she took it. Then she remembered who he was. The fog was lifting in her brain.

'You're the doctor from the hospital.'

'No, I was pretending to be the doctor from the hospital. I brought you here from your little rent-a-cockroach bedsit down in Carnwath. Near the farm where your son is being held.' He stood up straight. 'Let's face it, that place is nothing better than a farm with bars on the windows. Keeping the sick bastards inside. Protecting them. Because you know what people like me would do to your son if we caught them? We'd fucking hang them. Why should the taxpayer spend their hard-earned cash on that filth? Feed them, clothe them, medicate them, give them all the help they need. It would cost a lot less to put a bullet in their brains.'

Eve stared at the man, not daring to move. She

thought he was probably foaming at the mouth. He was obviously unhinged.

'Did you know that your husband is fucking the pathologist he works with?' the man said.

'What?'

He knelt down beside her, getting close. 'You left him, though, didn't you? His bed must have been very cold, so he got another woman in to warm it up. She stayed last night. While we were having our own fun, the slut stayed over.'

'You're lying,' Eve said, her voice catching in her throat.

Her hand moved fast, like a viper trying to strike, but something jarred her arm and her hand stopped before it got anywhere near him. She realised for the first time that her right wrist had a metal bracelet round it, and in turn, this was attached to a chain, which was attached to the wooden wall behind her.

The man laughed and stood up. 'That's a freebie. Next time, I'll take your bucket away and you can piss and shit yourself. The time after that, I'll break your fucking neck.'

He turned and walked away, then stopped at the wooden door. 'Eat your breakfast. I'll be back later. We have things to do.'

THIRTY-THREE

It looked like they had all teleported to the hospital in Dunfermline, the clock moving forward three hours. They were joined by Isla, who had insisted on coming along, knowing that Annie was going to be in the autopsy suite. Annie had told her things would be fine, as Davie Cook would be with her.

The mortuary was cool, a little too cool for Craig's liking, and he was glad he had a jacket on. A scarf would have been welcome. He was hungry now but didn't want to say anything.

'I'm fooking starving now,' Bailey said, and Craig silently thanked the man.

'If you lot want to go to the canteen, I'm sure they'll still have lunch going,' Annie said.

Nobody wanted to make the move.

'Biggie!' Bailey shouted, even though the man was standing behind him.

'Sir?'

'Go and get us some scran from the canteen. Isla, can you help him? We can have a little chow down in the break room.'

'Sure.'

They put their orders in, and retreated to the break room while Annie and Cook prepared the woman for the postmortem.

'Caitlin Morgan, aged thirty-six,' Craig said. 'Max is with Gary Menzies doing the death message. He sent me a text; she was married with two young boys.'

'Bastard,' Bailey said. 'I can't remember how old our victim was in Halifax, but I think she was in her thirties.'

'Our first one was in her twenties, then thirties, forties, fifties and sixties,' Craig said.

The food came in and Lance stood up to help. They sat round the table, batting ideas about.

'Was she chosen at random?' Bailey said. 'Our victim was taken at random, we think. We checked out the ex-husband, boyfriend, people she worked with, but there was nobody who jumped out. All of them had alibis for when she was taken.'

'I think he had to do some kind of homework,' Craig said. 'He had to be watching her, waiting for a chance to snatch her.'

'He managed to get close to her,' Biggie said. He looked at the others. 'Who would she trust? A copper.'

Craig nodded. 'Jack Bolton. We've put out a "be on the lookout" for him.'

'Did he drive up here?' Lance said. 'If so, the ANPR might have picked up his number.'

'We don't even know if he is up here,' Craig said. 'Let me make a phone call.' He excused himself and went out into the corridor before going into Annie's office.

He finally found the number he was looking for. He dialled it, feeling his heart racing a bit faster now.

'Mrs Bolton. Please don't hang up. It's DCI Craig.' He expected the call to be terminated immediately, but to his surprise, she didn't hang up.

'DCI Craig. What can I do for you?'

'I have a question to ask you, and it's of a sensitive nature.'

'Go on.'

'When your husband left, did he take his car?'

Silence for a moment before she answered. 'I don't know why you want that information, but no, he didn't. He took some clothes, put them in a bag and left.'

'My colleague Barry Norman said that you told him that Jack left around six months ago. Is that correct?'

'Only in part. Barry Norman didn't come here; his colleague Fred Kohler came here on his behalf. Nice gentleman.'

There was an awkward silence for a moment.

'Listen, Mrs Bolton –'

'Please don't. I feel bad enough as it is for spitting in your face. I don't know what came over me. I was angry the day of the funeral, but I wasn't just angry at you. I was angry at Sharon. For what she did.'

'What she did?'

'She was going to throw her whole career away. She told me and her father that she was quitting her job after the New Year and moving to Scotland with her new lover.'

Craig was silent. Maybe Mrs Bolton was of a generation that didn't approve of living together before marriage, but when he had seen her at the funeral, she hadn't looked that much older than he was.

'Her much *older* lover. He was retiring, she said, and they were planning to make a new life for themselves.'

'Oh. I didn't know.'

'Why would you know? I don't think she broadcasted it. She only told us because she had to, really. I was furious. She was a good-looking girl. She had Ronnie, but when I spoke to him, he said that she had dumped him a few months earlier. That's why he's a basket case now. He blames himself for her death. Said that if they had still been together, then he would have been able to protect her.'

'Does he know who the other man is?'

'No. Or if he does, he isn't saying. He tried repeatedly to talk sense into Sharon, but she had made up her mind. She was leaving for Scotland. Apparently, her boyfriend is Scottish. That's all I know. And that was enough to put her father over the edge. He told me before he left that he had found out who her boyfriend was, and he was going to go looking for the bastard. He was heading for Scotland. I thought it was an empty threat until he walked out and didn't contact me again.'

'And you haven't heard from him since?'

'Just the odd text. I tried calling, but he doesn't answer. He's hurting and he's looking for a solution. All he knew before he left was that they were going to Scotland, her boyfriend was a copper and he was going to retire. She was head over heels with this man, whoever he is.'

'I'm so sorry to hear that. I can only imagine.'

'You've got a lot on your plate up there. I don't blame you for what happened. I was just lashing out because I couldn't lash out at this new boyfriend she had. The cheeky bastard sent me a text. He said, "See you at the funeral. Mum."'

'Do you still have the number?'

'No. I erased it. But I had a feeling he was watching me.'

'Could it have been DCI Steve Carver? I know he retired and he was there at the funeral.'

'No, it wasn't him. Sharon couldn't stand him. Besides, I spoke to one of Ronnie's workmates, and he told me Carver was living in Spain. Whoever it was, it wasn't him.'

'Thank you for being so candid, Mrs Bolton.'

'Call me Edna. I'd like to call you Jimmy.'

'No problem.'

'Jimmy, next time you're down in London, pop in for a cup of tea. I'd like to chat about Sharon. I miss her so much and wish I hadn't given her so much grief.'

'We can't turn back the clock, Edna. Just think about the good memories you have of her.'

'I will. Thank you, Jimmy.'

He hung up and thought about a DI who had worked with Sharon and himself. Fred Kohler. It was name he couldn't forget. He'd liked the man. He looked at his contact list. He hadn't erased the names of his team from his phone when he moved up to Scotland. He looked up the number and dialled it.

'Sir! Good to hear from you,' Kohler said when he answered.

'How have you been?' Craig asked.

'Not too bad. Keeping busy. And now I'm running about on the weekend, but it doesn't matter. Sometimes we have to go above and beyond.'

'I heard you went to look at some records in the storage facility.'

'I did indeed. This case with Starman coming back is awful.'

'You saw Jack Bolton's name on the sign-in book, didn't you?' Craig asked.

'I did.'

'Did you recognise any other names from our team?'

Kohler paused for a moment. 'One or two, which is to be expected.' He told Craig which names.

'Thanks, Fred. You've been a great help.'

They chatted for a few more seconds before Craig hung up.

Then he went back to the others.

THIRTY-FOUR

It was past dinnertime when the postmortem was finished and they had all left. Raymond Taylor was bringing down a young woman who had passed away after a road accident.

'See? Motorbikes are dangerous. My old mother used to say that. She still does. Nag, nag, nag. But at least you had a go. To feel that magnificent beast under you, getting up to speed in a flash. That must have been fantastic. Not the dying part, though. No, that must have hurt. I heard that your boyfriend died on impact. He was in charge, though, wasn't he? Selfish bastard. You were on the back, holding on for dear life no doubt. A car pulled across in front of you and he hit it doing sixty. You were lucky to survive for a week.'

He pushed her out of the lift and pulled the cover back in place. Just in case. You never knew who was hanging about here.

The office lights were out and there was no sign of anybody.

'See, if you had gone out with me, we would have had a car to drive in.' He pulled the cover back. 'Would you have liked that?'

Donna smiled at him. 'Yes, I would have loved that. Cars are safer. What kind of car do you have?'

'A Porsche 911.' He held up a hand. 'Don't worry, I wouldn't have driven it like a maniac. It's one of the classic ones. You have to take care of the classics. Be gentle with them. You would love it.'

'That sounds fantastic. If I wasn't...'

'With Cameron? I know. But he died on impact. Broken neck, I heard. You won't have to worry about him. I'll take care of you. You'll want for nothing. Come and live with me in my big house down by the sea. Did I tell you I have a sea view? It's beautiful. You're going to be excited by it. And of course, you'll have your own car. I don't own a motorcycle. They're for idiots. Organ donors, as my old ma says. And true, in the case of Cameron. Where did his heart and lungs go? I wonder. I heard they took his eyes too. I'm no surgeon, but eyes? Still, they must know what they're doing.'

He stopped the gurney at one of the fridge drawers and opened it. He transferred her to the steel tray and slid her in. 'It was nice chatting with you.'

He closed the door and was about to turn back to the gurney when he felt something go round his neck.

And then he was being lifted off his feet.

THIRTY-FIVE

Craig had got used to not cooking at the weekends. Saturday and Sunday were for having food delivered, and tonight was no exception. He had called for Indian and now he and Annie were sitting at the dining table.

'I appreciate you letting me stay here,' she said. 'I mean, I'm not scared to go home, obviously.'

'Obviously. You don't want to be parted from me, that's all.'

He was just tucking into his korma – he didn't want his arse on fire later, he'd explained – when his phone rang.

'Sorry. Hazard of the job,' he said.

'You don't have to apologise. To me especially.'

He stood up from the dining table and took the phone into another room.

'It's Tom Bailey. Sorry to disturb you, pal. Me and the lad are having a McDonald's in Dunfermline. I like this place. It's next to a Tesco, but other than that, I'm fooked if I know where we are.'

'It's no problem, Tom.'

'Listen, I was thinking about your victim from today. I called a pal of mine who worked the case in Halifax. He said that the first victim was a nurse, just like today. But here's where the difference is: our second victim was killed three months later, not a year later. And she was the second and last one. She was also a teacher. I think your guy will strike again, and I think she's going to be a teacher, just like your original victim, back in the day.'

'Christ. I wonder why he didn't wait a year?' Craig said.

'Halifax wasn't his hunting ground. He killed there, but he lived in London. He came there for a reason, as yet unknown. I think he had family there.'

'That's a possibility,' Craig said.

'Like my wife. She's not a Yorkshire lass, but I don't hold that against her. She's a southern git, like Biggie.'

'Hey, I heard that,' Craig heard the young DS say. 'I'm sitting right here.'

'But anyway,' Bailey continued, 'we go down there to visit her family. Bunch of fooking inbreds, but I love 'em. What if your London guy was in the same position as me, but in reverse? He lived in London, but his wife came from Yorkshire. He travelled up with her and somehow went out and killed women.'

'That's good thinking, Tom. I never thought of that.'

'Just batting ideas about, lad. But anyway, are you up for a pint tonight? I can only watch so many shows about fooking old cars being sold.'

Craig laughed. 'We could have a pint at the Pitreavie Golf Club. It's where a bunch of us usually drink if we want peace and quiet.'

'And I bet it's fooking cheap too. Right up my alley. Since the lad here's paying.'

Biggie said something that Craig couldn't quite hear.

'About an hour? We're having a quick dinner first at the Golden Arches.'

'See you there, pal.'

Craig hung up and went back to the dining table. 'That was Tom Bailey. He's treating Biggie to dinner, so they're in a McDonald's that's next to a Tesco, he says.'

Annie thought for a moment. 'Turnstone Road, probably. That's next to Tesco.'

'You and your fine dining. Of course you would know where it is.' He laughed. 'He wants to go for a pint. We're meeting at the golf club. You up for it?'

'To be honest, Jim, I'm bushed. Would you mind if I stayed here and kept Finn company?'

'That's fine. I won't be long.'

She smiled. 'You don't have to explain to me.'

They finished dinner and Craig loaded the dishwasher. He kissed her goodbye and patted Finn's head. The dog was lying down chewing a soft toy and gave his tail a couple of thumps.

Craig had called for a taxi and was in the golf club twenty minutes later, just as Bailey and Biggie walked in.

'There you are, lad. Biggie here says his money's burning a hole in his wallet.'

'He's paraphrasing, of course,' Biggie said. 'Sir? What you for?'

'Pint of lager, thanks.'

'We'll be at a table,' Bailey said. 'Try not to spill any of mine.'

They sat down, facing the bar.

'None of your mates coming along tonight, then?' Bailey asked.

Craig looked at him. 'It's usually just Dan and Isla. I didn't ask either of them. It being a Sunday.'

'I don't usually drink on a Sunday either, but the lad insisted.'

Biggie brought three pints across.

'Cheers, son,' Craig said.

'Cheers, lad.'

They all clinked glasses.

'Did you think any more about what I said?' Bailey asked Craig. 'About my theory – somebody in London having a wife from Yorkshire?'

'I did. It's a good theory. But how do we check?'

Bailey put his pint down. 'You have a point.'

Biggie looked at them. 'What if it was somebody you knew? Somebody who was part of the investigation. Somebody who would have intimate knowledge of the crimes. Do you know anybody like that?'

'None of my team had a wife from Yorkshire,' Craig said. Then his phone dinged. 'Excuse me, lads.'

He took his phone out while Bailey and Biggie began arguing over whether Bailey should have bought more chocolate from the Tesco next to McDonald's. Craig looked at his phone. It was a text from Eve. He opened it up and stared at the screen, not quite believing his own eyes.

'Oh fuck,' he said.

'What's wrong, lad?' Bailey asked.

Craig showed him the photo of a woman who was chained to a wooden wall, a gag in her mouth. A London A–Z on her lap.

'Who's that?' Bailey asked.

'My wife,' Craig answered. 'The Atlas Killer's next victim.'

THIRTY-SIX

Annie was settling down to watch a show about antiques when her phone dinged. She thought it would be Craig calling her, asking her to go and fetch him. She'd said she would, but he'd only been gone an hour.

She read the text: *There's an emergency at the hospital. Raymond's dead.*

Christ. She assumed it was Raymond Taylor.

Finn stopped chewing his toy and looked at her.

'I won't be long, boy. I have to go out for a little bit. I'll text your dad.'

She grabbed her car keys and left. The sun was still out and it was a beautiful night. Maybe she and Craig could take a walk down by the shore with Finn later on.

It didn't take her long to drive to the hospital. She used the car's entertainment system to send Craig the text.

She parked at the mortuary entrance and used her pass to gain entry. She was a bit apprehensive, but the hospital was full of people, she told herself.

But none of them were down here.

She'd expected to see police cars outside, but there were none. Maybe the officers had come through the main entrance.

She walked along the back corridor, once again expecting to see activity, but there was none. She could see her office, on the left now, as she was coming from the opposite direction from the lifts. The lights were on in there. Maybe cleaning staff?

'Hello?' she said.

No answer.

She approached the office and looked in through the window and saw a box of chocolates on the desk. Was that the same box as before? No, this one was different.

She walked up to the rubber doors and pushed her way in. Walked through to the refrigeration area.

Raymond Taylor was hanging by a rope around his neck, his feet well off the ground. She walked forward when she saw a piece of paper lying on the floor. She picked it up and read it. There was one word printed on it in black marker.

Sorry.

There was no police activity because nobody had called them, she realised.

Then the rubber doors bumped closed behind her as somebody else came in.

'Hello, Annie.'

'Christ, Annie, no,' Craig said out loud when he read her text message.

'What's wrong?' Bailey asked.

'It's Annie, the pathologist. She sent me a text. She's being stalked by somebody. She's been sent chocolates and flowers and cards, things like that. Now she's had a text saying the guy we thought might be stalking her, somebody who works in the hospital, is dead.'

Bailey looked at Craig. 'You think it's real?'

'I think somebody is trying to get her to the hospital on her own.'

'Fook me. How far is it from here?'

'Ten minutes.'

'Let's fooking go. Biggie, you're driving, so don't drive like a drunken coont.'

But Biggie wasn't listening; he was already on his feet and marching towards the car park. He had the engine running by the time the two older detectives got in the car.

'There's her car there,' Craig said, still thinking about Eve being tied up. His heart was racing. He wanted to find her, but he was still trying to find out where she was. He knew where Annie was.

'There's her car,' he said, pointing to the Audi.

The back door to the mortuary was locked.

'How the fook do we get in?'

'This way,' Craig said.

They rounded the mortuary building, to where the kitchens were located. A man wearing a jacket over his chef's uniform was standing there smoking a cigarette.

'Hey, you!' Craig shouted, running up to him.

'I'm finished. I've already clocked out. I know I shouldn't smoke, but I'm waiting for Mary...'

'We just need in here, son,' Craig said, running

past the man into the kitchens, Bailey and Biggie in tow.

A woman was walking towards them. 'Which way to the mortuary?' Craig asked her.

She pointed. 'Through that door, turn right, then right again.'

The three men ran through the kitchens, dodging round steel tables, and left through the door. They turned right into the corridor, then right again. It brought them into the corridor where the lifts were. Annie's office was lit up, on their right, in the distance.

'Christ, I hope we're not too late,' Craig said.

When they reached her office, Davie Cook was sitting there doing paperwork.

'Where is she, Davie?' Craig asked.

'Who?'

'The woman you've been stalking,' Bailey said.

'Where the fuck's Annie?' Craig said.

'What are you talking about, stalking her?' Cook said, standing up.

'We thought it was Raymond Taylor. You made a good case for it. Made us think he was daft.'

'He is daft. He talks to the dead.'

'But he wasn't stalking Annie. *You* are. It makes sense: you work with her, you're attracted to her. You sent her a text saying Raymond's dead. Where are they? Or was that just pish you were talking?'

'You're making a fool of yourself, sir. I know nothing about that. Let me show you.' Cook came round from the desk. 'She isn't here. I was just finishing up the paperwork.'

They walked into the corridor and through into the fridge area.

'See? Nobody here.'

They looked around. Nothing. No sign of Annie.

'Her car's in the car park,' Craig said.

'Is it? I haven't seen her. Now, gentlemen, I have to lock up. If you wouldn't mind leaving.'

'Shut the fook up,' Bailey said. 'We're not going any-fooking-where until you tell us where she is.'

'You've looked around. Maybe she's upstairs talking to a doctor.'

Craig heard a muffled thump. 'What was that?'

'Well, now, thanks for calling round, gents, but if you could now move out in an orderly fashion,' Cook said, his voice raised.

'Watch him,' Craig said, and started pulling on drawer handles.

'Help him, Biggie!' Bailey said, and the younger man also started pulling on drawers.

Cook turned to run and Bailey grabbed hold of

him by the hair. 'Believe me when I say I will rip your fooking bollocks off.'

Cook squealed as Bailey pulled his hair tighter.

Annie was in a bottom drawer, bound and gagged. Craig felt his heart explode with panic, or what felt like a slight heart attack, he wasn't sure which. He fought to compose himself as he hurriedly reached down and got her to her feet. He took the gag out of her mouth and Biggie untied her hands. They had been bound with a torn sheet, like her ankles had been.

'Bastard,' she spat. 'Raymond Taylor was hanging from one of the top doors. I think he killed him.'

'Annie, listen,' Cook said in a pleading voice. 'We can be together. I'll look after you. I'll protect you. I've loved you from afar. I just wanted to scare you so I could protect you.'

Annie walked over and kicked him square in the nuts. 'You bastard. I should cut your fucking throat for doing that to me. I trusted you.'

But Cook wasn't listening. Bailey had let go of his hair and let him collapse to the floor.

'Uniforms are on their way,' Craig said, holding Annie. 'We called it in from the car.'

'Thank you all.'

Biggie was cuffing Cook's hands behind his back.

'We can't read him his rights, sir,' he said to Craig, who obliged.

A couple of minutes later, uniforms rushed in and took Cook away.

Craig's phone dinged. He took it out and looked at the text. 'I still have a problem,' Craig said to Annie. He showed her the photo of Eve. 'I had Max do me a favour this afternoon. He just found the answer for me and sent me the text with the details. I think I know where Eve's being held.'

'By Jack Bolton?' she asked.

'No. Not him.'

THIRTY-SEVEN

Craig drove his car along the rutted track that might have been a road at one time, but the years hadn't been kind to it.

The farm couldn't be seen from the road, which gave them an advantage, but if they stormed right up to it, then *he* would have the advantage.

Bailey was lying down on the back seat of the Volvo. 'This would be so much more comfortable if I wasn't such a fat bastard.'

The farmhouse was over on the right, down the hill a bit, and the stables were on the left.

'They used to have horses, Jack Bolton's family, before the farm went sideways,' Craig said.

He pulled around the side of the stables, slowing the car down. Bailey opened the back door and got out, keeping low as he closed the door without banging it. Then Craig turned the car round and headed back round to the front where he parked. He turned the engine off and walked inside. He had his extendable baton out, just in case. Each stall he passed was empty, until he reached the last one. That was where he found the body.

Jack Bolton had one hand chained to the boards. His face was white and it looked like he had been dead for a while. There were scratches on one cheek, as if a woman had lashed out with her fingernails. Craig checked for a pulse just to make sure, and didn't find one. He heard movement and looked up. Bailey was standing there watching him.

'Is that him?'

Craig shook his head. 'No. That's Jack Bolton. He was just a pawn.'

Then a text came in from Biggie: *Trojan*. He was out of sight with Max Hold, Isla and Gary Menzies. The uniforms were there in force too, but well out of sight.

'He's coming.'

They saw headlight beams cut through the darkness, and they looked out of one of the dirty windows and saw the car heading towards the house.

Craig shot off a text to Biggie: *Going to the house. Give us two, then bring the cavalry.*

They sneaked out the back of the stables, keeping low, Bailey as low as he could comfortably manage.

The car was parked in front of the house, the lights off. Now lights were on in the house in what would be the living room, Craig assumed.

They got to the front door and were about to enter when it opened.

'Christ,' the man at the door said, and Craig grabbed hold of him. He shoved him back into the hallway and all the way into the living room, where he threw him into a chair.

'Fuck me, Jimmy, that's being a bit rough, isn't it?' the man said.

'Where is she?'

Barry Norman smiled at him. 'Who?'

'Don't fuck with me. I want to know where Eve is.'

'Well, I don't have to worry about that, because I know where the love of my life is: in the fucking ground.' Now Norman wasn't smiling as he jumped up. 'Your son took Sharon away from me. We were going to come and live up here.' He pointed a finger at Craig.

Bailey was standing there watching, waiting to break the man into small pieces.

'See this place, Jimmy? This was Sharon's. Her dad signed it over to her.'

'I know. I had somebody check the Land Registry.'

'We were going to come up here and get married. But your son changed all that, didn't he?' Norman sneered at Craig. 'You didn't even see that, because you're a shite copper. I wanted to show everybody just how shite you are. You couldn't find those other killers back then, and you couldn't catch them now. That's what they would think: the killers are back and DCI James Craig still can't catch them.' He looked at Bailey. 'Who the fuck are you?'

'I'll ask you to show me some respect, ya little bastard. But for your information, I'm DCI Bailey. From Yorkshire. Where your killer struck.'

'This has nothing to do with you, then, pal. So be on your fucking way.'

'I asked him here. He's a consultant. Now tell me where Eve is.' Craig took a step towards Norman.

'You're the bright spark, you tell me where she is. You seem to have figured it out this far. How did you do that? Entertain us.'

'I made a few phone calls. If it was a copycat,

then he had to have known the inside information. It had to be a copper. He would have had to have gone to records and looked up the case file. Jack Bolton was in there, but so were you. I spoke to Fred Kohler. He told me.'

'That was a risk, I admit.'

'I also spoke to Edna Bolton. She told me about Sharon leaving the force and heading to Scotland, where she was going to live with her much older lover.'

'I don't believe you.'

'I don't fucking care if you believe me. Edna told me she was angry with me, but she was also angry with Sharon for throwing her life away. We're friends now.'

'How very cosy.'

'Where's Eve?' Craig asked again.

'Figure it out yourself.'

'You wrote the letters, didn't you?' Craig said. 'Pretending they were from Jack Bolton.'

Norman smiled. 'See? You can work things out when you try.'

They heard vehicles screeching to a halt outside, then suddenly the house was filled with stamping boots. Biggie, Isla, and the others came in.

Uniforms rushed inside, and Bailey gave them

orders to search every inch of the house for the missing woman.

DSup Mark Baker walked in. 'Is this the prick here?' he said.

'Hey, cheeky bastard. Who are you?' Norman said.

'DSup Baker.'

'I was the same rank as you, pal, but in a far better force.'

'Shut up.'

Too late, Craig caught movement from the corner of his eye. Norman was far enough away for him not to do any damage to Craig, but he could do damage to himself.

He took the knife and sliced the top of the inside of his thigh. Blood spurted out as Bailey grabbed hold of the knife hand and yanked the weapon out of it.

'Femoral artery,' Norman said. 'Going to be with Sharon.'

Blood shot out of the wound like a fountain. Craig looked around and saw a blanket on the back of a chair and shoved it against the wound. Bailey took his belt off and wrapped it around the top of Norman's leg, creating a makeshift tourniquet.

It was no good. Norman had opened up the artery quite a bit.

He was turning white. He put a hand round the back of Craig's head, gently pulling him towards his face.

'You can find Eve. You can work it out.' Then he slipped away.

Craig stood up and wanted to shout and kick the man, but he knew he had to keep a clear head.

Annie came in. 'Oh, Christ,' she said, moving towards Norman. She knelt down, but knew he was gone.

Bailey took his belt back and looped it through his trousers after wiping it on Norman's jacket.

'Where was the first Atlas victim found in Yorkshire?' Craig asked Bailey.

Baker went out of the room to make sure the uniforms were tearing the place apart.

'By the River Calder. Sitting with her back against a tree, looking out towards the water.'

'Like our victim today. Propped against the rock. What about the second?'

'At the old Jubilee Colliery. It's a museum now, but it was a wreck back then. Why, are there any collieries around here?'

'Plenty, but he would have chosen one where he wouldn't be seen.'

'I know where there's such a place,' Annie said.

THIRTY-EIGHT

St Ninian's Former Opencast Mine was now a place for dog walkers.

'It's just outside Kelty, about ten minutes from here if we boot it,' Annie said.

They were outside Kinross, only a few minutes away from the motorway.

They rushed to their cars, and Mark Baker told some of the uniforms to pull out all the stops and get a fucking crack on.

A small convoy fired off the farm and was on the motorway heading south minutes later. The blue lights cut through the darkness, and cars made way for the police vehicles. They came off at Kelty, and turned right and stopped at the entrance to the mine. Gates barred their way, until a uniform jumped out with bolt cutters and cut the padlock. Then they were in.

They drove through the darkness until they came to a huge mound with a track running round it, ascending to the top. It was known as The Walnut Whips.

There was an avenue at the top, a pathway flanked at either side by rusty pieces of former mining equipment, wheels and buckets that had once hung on the front of diggers.

Torches cut through the pitch black. This was what Craig would remember later on. The torchlight, the shouts, the noise. Somebody yelling, *'Over here!'*

He would remember Annie running forward with her black bag of magic tricks. Sometimes he forgot she was a doctor as well as a pathologist.

He would remember the smell of the summer air, fresh and cool.

He would remember seeing a figure lying in one of the rusty heavy machinery buckets.

He wouldn't remember much more than that. And somebody saying, *'We found her.'*

THIRTY-NINE

The next day

'She's lost a lot of blood, but she'll pull through,' the surgeon told Craig. 'She's sleeping now but you can come back later and see her if you want to.'

'That's good. I will.'

Annie was by his side. 'You should go in alone and see her when you come back,' she said.

'You saved her life,' Craig said. 'You stopped the bleeding.'

'I know. You owe me big time.' She smiled at him. 'I'll leave you to it. I know you'll have a lot to talk about.' She was about to walk away when he gently grabbed her arm.

'She doesn't want me. She made that clear. Her life is Joe now. I wanted to find her like I would have wanted to find any victim.'

'I know.'

'I have to go now. Tom and Biggie are waiting downstairs. We have one more thing to do.'

'Is it going to be dangerous? Will I have to change my underwear later on?'

'Only if you want to.' He leaned down and kissed her gently on the lips before walking away.

'I bet you do that to all the doctors,' she called after him.

'Only the good-looking ones.'

Then he was in the lift and gone.

In the lobby, Bailey and Biggie were waiting.

'You ready, boys?'

'As we'll ever be,' Bailey said.

They went out into the sunshine and got into Craig's car. They drove down the M90 and took the slip road for North Queensferry. Craig navigated to the hotel.

Lance Harrison was waiting on the steps with his suitcase.

'This sure is a fine view,' he said, pointing to the new Queensferry Crossing bridge.

'It's fantastic,' Craig agreed. 'Before we take you

to the airport, there's one thing I'd like your opinion on, if that's okay?'

'Sure. It won't take long, though, will it?' the pathologist said. 'I don't want to miss my flight.'

'Don't you worry about your flight,' Bailey said. 'Biggie, get the man's luggage.'

Biggie took the case and put it in the boot of the car, then the young detective got in beside Craig while Lance sat in the back next to Bailey.

Craig headed out to the motorway, but instead of heading south towards the airport, he headed north.

'I think you're going the wrong way, Jim,' Lance said, a slightly worried look on his face now.

'No, I'm going the right way, Lance. Unfortunately, we're heading for Glenrothes, not the airport.'

'Why? What's going on?'

Craig looked in the mirror. 'I called you Lance. Maybe I should have called you Starman. Or maybe you'd prefer your other moniker, The Atlas Killer.'

'What the hell is this?' Lance said, leaning forward, but Bailey put a hand on his chest. Lance sat back.

'It took us twenty years, but we got you in the end. It feels good. What do you say, Tom?'

'It does. After all this time, it feels good to have the killer in the back of a car.'

'Turn this fucking car around and take me to the airport.'

'You're going to be booked in after we charge you with murder.' Again, Craig looked in the mirror. 'Lance Harrison, I'm arresting you for the murder of...'

Craig rattled off the names of the victims.

'You're an asshole.'

'It was one little detail all those years ago that let you down. If it hadn't been for that, you might have got away with it,' Craig said.

Lance stared at Craig's eyes in the rearview, but he didn't say a word.

'You want to know what it was?'

'Fuck you.'

'Pants. You see, when Barry Norman started killing, he put the tarot card in their pants. He put the map in the nurse's pants. He didn't work the original cases, so he had to read the reports to get the inside details. Like the wristwatch and the tarot card. In the postmortem reports, you mentioned that the cards and the maps were put in their pants. But being an American, "pants" means something else to you. Trousers. The tarot cards were put in their trouser pockets. I knew that, because I worked the cases. But Barry didn't. He thought you literally meant underpants, so he put the cards there. Only an American would say pants for trousers. That's what made me think of you. You did the original post-mortems on the victims. Even though the forensics reports said trousers, yours said pants.'

'We did a little background research,' Bailey said, 'and found out your wife came from Oldham. Which isn't that far from Halifax. That's why you killed when you were there. Couldn't you help yourself? Maybe we would never have put two and two together if you'd just stuck to killing in London.'

Lance laughed. 'Kept you fooled for all these years, didn't I? Twenty years. That was some run.'

'You didn't just kill twenty years ago and then stop, did you?' Craig said.

'You work it out, Jimmy. You work it out.'

FORTY

Three weeks later

Finn was standing by Craig's side when Annie walked up with three ice cream cones. The fairground was still on the Burntisland Links and it was still busy. Two girls being abducted from the fair didn't seem to faze anybody. Such was life now, Craig thought. People were being desensitised by all the violence online. You could watch videos of car crashes, road rage attacks, animals eating each other. Whatever your pleasure.

'There you go,' Annie said, handing Craig a cone.

'Thanks,' he said. They were on the promenade,

and Craig was sitting on a bench, looking out to sea. Annie sat down and gave Finn his cone before eating hers. Craig gave her a paper hanky from his backpack to wipe off the ice cream that had run down the side of her hand.

'Eve's back down in Carnwath now?' she asked.

'She's settled in again. She said she'll buy a small place. We have savings, money from the sale of the house in London. I'll buy her out from this house in Dalgety Bay. Her uncle left us it, but she wants me to have my half, so I'll buy her out. There'll still be money left over.'

'What about Finn?' The dog was lapping at his cone.

'She said he can stay with me. She wouldn't be able to give him the attention he needs. She's concentrating on Joe right now. She wants to come and visit him now and again, and that's fine.'

Annie looked out to sea through her big brown sunglasses. 'What about us, Jimmy? Where do we go from here?' She turned to face him.

He leaned in and gave her a kiss.

AFTERWORD

I hope you enjoyed this latest James Craig novel. Now, let me put this to rest. Some of you might have finished this book and are now thinking, "Wait a minute. I just finished a book by another author who has a detective dating a pathologist. Are you copying, John?" The answer is, yes. Copying myself. You see, I did it first. A detective dating a pathologist, in my DI Frank Miller books. The first one, Crash Point, came out nearly ten years ago. Sometimes books have a habit of writing themselves, or at least, partly.

When I first started writing the James Craig books, I had him happily married, but I threw a wrench in the works of their marriage. The character's lives evolve as each book comes out, and this one

AFTERWORD

was no different. I had Eve wanting to live closer to the psychiatric hospital, but Craig didn't want to move. That happened between books, so in this book, we catch up with them. Eve has moved and they are now separated. I didn't start out the book with the intention of Craig having a relationship with Annie. It just happened. Will they be together in the next book? We shall see.

As usual, I would like to thank some people: Lisa and Gary, my friends in Scotland. My family, for picking up the slack in the background. My two writing buddies, Bear and Bella, who make this writing journey a little less solitary. To Jacqueline Beard, who has a skill I can only dream about. To my friend, who is always available with an answer and who has the patience of a saint. And to my friend Spence.

And to you, the reader. I appreciate each and every one of you.

If you could please leave a rating or a review of this book, that would be fantastic. Every one helps.

If anybody would like to contact me, please feel free. Questions about the books, or tips on writing, just not questions like, what is your social security number? You can contact me through my website and I'll get back to you as soon as.

www.johncarsonauthor.com

Until the next time, stay safe my friends.

ABOUT THE AUTHOR

John Carson is originally from Edinburgh, Scotland, but now lives with his wife and family in New York State. And two dogs. And four cats.

www.johncarsonauthor.com

Printed in Great Britain
by Amazon